A Single Bead

a single bead

By Stephanie Engelman

Pauline
BOOKS & MEDIA
Boston

Library of Congress Cataloging-in-Publication Data

Engelman, Stephanie, author.
  A single bead / by Stephanie Engelman.
     pages cm
  Summary: A year after her grandmother's death in an airplane crash, Katelyn
and her family visit the field where it happened, and Kate finds a single bead from
her grandmother's rosary, and as more beads show up, Kate learns that people
are crediting the beads with saving their lives--but can the story of the miraculous
beads can save Kate's mother from the depression that is ruining her life?
  ISBN 978-0-8198-9054-2 (pbk.) -- ISBN 0-8198-9054-5 (pbk.) 1. Rosary--Ju-
venile fiction. 2. Beads--Religious aspects--Catholic Church--Juvenile fiction.
3. Bereavement--Juvenile fiction. 4. Grief--Juvenile fiction. 5. Families--Juvenile
fiction. 6. Depression, Mental--Juvenile fiction. [1. Rosary--Fiction. 2. Beads--Re-
ligious aspects--Fiction. 3. Grief--Fiction. 4. Family life--Fiction. 5. Depression,
Mental--Fiction. 6. Catholics--Fiction. 7. Christian life--Fiction.] I. Title.
  PZ7.1.E53Si 2016
  813.6--dc23
  [Fic]

2015020764

This is a work of fiction. Names, characters, places, events, and incidents are either the products of the author's imagination or used in a fictitious manner. Any resemblance to actual persons, living or dead, or actual events is purely coincidental.

Many manufacturers and sellers distinguish their products through the use of trademarks. Any trademarked designations that appear in this book are used in good faith but are not authorized by, associated with, or sponsored by the trademark owners.

Cover & book design by Mary Joseph Peterson, FSP

Cover photo © Darius Strazdas—Dreamstime.com

"P" and PAULINE are registered trademarks of the Daughters of St. Paul.

Copyright © 2016, Stephanie Engelman

Published by Pauline Books & Media, 50 Saint Pauls Avenue, Boston, MA 02130–3491

Printed in the U.S.A.

www.pauline.org

Pauline Books & Media is the publishing house of the Daughters of St. Paul, an international congregation of women religious serving the Church with the communications media.

3 4 5 6 7 8 9   22 21 20 19 18

For Dave and Mary Ann Lear

When I wrote about
the very best grandparents imaginable,
it was only natural
that they would be so much like you.

"By praying the Rosary, those in heaven and on
earth share their feelings, words, and actions."

—attributed to Saint John XXIII, pope from 1958–1963

My feet squish in the mud as I shift my weight, glancing around at the family members gathered in the bare farm field. I wish someone would just speak up and say something. Anything. A nice memory, something they miss, a funny thing she said . . . maybe just that she's in a better place now. But somehow we all just stand here, waiting.

The sun is struggling to peek through heavy clouds that, only a few minutes ago, dumped buckets of water on the field where we now stand. I'm just glad it stopped, or else I'm sure Aunt Mary Ellen would have insisted that we brave the rain to honor Grandma. Being here is hard enough. Getting pelted with rain in the cool air of early spring would have added a whole new dimension of awful.

Finally, Uncle Joseph clears his throat, his Adam's apple bobbing against his starched Roman collar. We should have made bets on who'd talk first. I knew it'd be him. Mom lets a sob escape, then closes her mouth hard, scrunches up her face, and presses her fist against her lips. It's weird to see her like this, though I guess I'm getting used to it. I always thought she was so strong—my rock, the one who always had it under control, always knew the right answer. But ever since Grandma died she seems lost, weak, and totally unsure of herself. I wonder what I'd be like if *she* died? I guess I'll probably find out someday.

Uncle Joseph glances around at the faces of his brothers and sisters, their spouses, and his nieces and nephews, and begins. "Mom would be so happy to see all of us here together. I remember when I was, well, probably a freshmen or sophomore in high school—around Kate and Evelyn's age." He motions to me and my cousin Evelyn, who's standing with her family, next to mine.

Uncle Joseph chuckles. "Matthew caught me playing his guitar, rockin' out to Pearl Jam. I had broken a string. He was so ticked, he threatened to tell my girlfriend about the time—" Uncle Matthew elbows him in the ribs and he changes tracks. "Anyways . . . we wound up on the floor throwing punches, until Mom came in. She never even raised her voice. Just crossed her arms and cleared her throat. This wasn't the first fight she'd broken up between the two of us that week. She waited until we stopped, put her hands on her hips, and said, 'Boys, you will always have people in your lives that you have a difficult time getting along with. That's just part of life. But *you two*'"—Uncle Joseph stabs a finger at the air in front of him—"'*You two are brothers. You are family.*' She told us we didn't have a choice about getting along, and let us know in no uncertain terms that we'd better figure it out, and figure it out quick, because she wasn't going to have any more of *this*—" He waves his hand at the ground in front of him. "She was right, though. One day, we actually did figure out that we loved each other. And we've been best friends ever since. Just like she always used to say: 'If you can't love your family—'"

Uncle Matthew breaks in, and they chorus together: "'—you can't love anyone at all!'"

A soft rumble of laughter floats across the field as the brothers and sisters, seven of them in all, share in the memory. The mood is finally lightened. Aunt Mary Ellen's rosary beads might be spared from total annihilation. If they were made of coal, I'm pretty sure she'd have turned them into diamonds by now. Even Mom, who never smiles anymore, manages a watery smirk when her big brother, Uncle David, puts an arm around her shoulders. I try not to feel jealous when she returns his hug.

Now everybody starts sharing memories: how Grandma loved to cook, but so frequently screwed up the recipes; how she loved to garden, and *always* got *that* right; the time she totally freaked out when a snake slithered in through the basement door; the way she seemed to make it to every grandkid's game, like she could bilocate or something; the fact that she took such good care of Papa when he was sick, and kept ironing his jeans, right up to the last day. Seriously. Who ever heard of ironing jeans? But that was Grandma.

She was pretty awesome.

One thing nobody talks about. Nobody talks about the sunny morning a year ago today, when her plane dropped out of the sky. Nobody mentions that she was headed to Colorado to visit Aunt Liz, or that we heard it on the news before we knew that it was Grandma's plane. Nobody talks about waiting for hours to find out if she was gone. Nobody looks at this field and says, "This is it. This is where the plane went down. This is all we have left of Grandma."

Which seems like the elephant in the room—or on the farm field, I guess I should say. It's why we're all here, after all. But I guess everybody's had enough crying and now they want to try to be happy.

I glance away from my own family, toward another cluster of people standing in the distance. They're here for the same reason, I'm sure, and I wonder about who *they* lost. Maybe a grandmother or grandfather, or both. Or maybe it was a teenager, like me. Thinking about it sends a shiver down my spine. All those people, headed for a vacation or business trip or on their way home from one, and then all of a sudden it was over.

Is that family trying to move on, too? Are they trying to be happy? Is it working?

Uncle Joseph starts to pray a Rosary. He says that's what Grandma would have wanted us to do, and he's probably right. But Grandma prayed a lot of Rosaries, and look where it got her. So I walk away. I don't know where I'm headed, until I stop watching my feet and look up to see a group of trees on the other side of the field. Another step, I unglue my feet from the muck and start heading toward them. Step by sticky, squelchy step, it's like I'm totally mesmerized by these trees and just have to keep walking. I hear Uncle Joseph droning on behind me, "Hail Mary, full of grace . . ." and everyone else joining in, "Holy Mary, Mother of God, pray for us sinners now and at the hour of our death."

I wonder if she did? Pray for Grandma at the hour of her death? I hope so. I don't like to think about what it must have been like—when Grandma died—but I imagine she could have used all the prayers she could get.

I keep walking toward the trees, and it's almost like I'm being drawn by some kind of invisible force. Once I enter under their canopy, the muck ends, and is replaced by a grassy bed peppered with wild flowers. The wind rustles the leaves, and droplets of water rain gently on my face. I drag a sleeve across my wet cheeks, but stop suddenly when a tiny gleam of light catches my eye. There's something nestled among the tiny purple flowers at my feet.

Stooping down to push the flowers aside, I discover a small, silver bead, and my heart flutters.

It's not possible. The investigators were all over this field, looking for every scrap they could possibly find. How could this have been left behind? I'm having a hard time breathing, and tears blur my vision. I wipe them away, because I have to see this. I have to hold it, touch it—feel the ridges of the letters imprinted on three sides, and run my nail along the cross on the fourth. Everything I am zones into that tiny little bead. . . . It's just a little fragment of a piece of jewelry, right?

But it's not. It's a bead from Grandma's rosary. And not just any bead. My bead.

K M R. Katelyn Marie Roberts. That's me. Who else could it be?

I start to shake, and I sink to my knees. I feel the sobs coming up out of me before they rip from my lips. It can't be. It can't be. It. Just. Can't.

I can still hear the drone of the Hail Marys behind me, but I can't make out the words. I kneel on the wet grass, crying, wondering, not understanding. I don't know how much time has passed, but Dad must have seen me wandering into the woods and known something was wrong. I hear his voice from far off, and then suddenly his hand is on my shoulder, giving it a gentle squeeze.

"Kate, are you okay?"

I fold the bead into my hand and wipe my face with my jacket sleeve again, only this time to wipe away the tears. I look up at Dad and try to pretend that I'm fine. Of course, he knows that I'm not, but that's to be expected here, today. I roll off my knees and sit down on the soggy ground, staring blindly toward the group in the field. Dad joins me, sitting on his jacket to stay dry. I feel the water soaking through my skirt, but I don't care. He puts his arm around me and we just sit there, listening to the drone of the Rosary prayers coming at us across the soaked earth.

Finally, they're done. Aunt Mary Ellen places a white cross in the ground, and several of my aunts and uncles lay flowers around it. Then they start to break up, heading to their cars. Mom looks toward me and Dad, but doesn't come any closer to us. She probably doesn't want to mess up her shoes by walking through the mud. She definitely doesn't want to have to deal with her daughter's messy emotions.

Dad yells that we'll be right there, but doesn't make any move to get up.

After a few more minutes, I give a final sniffle and stand up, discreetly tucking the bead into the pocket of my coat. I don't tell Dad. I don't know why, but it feels like my little secret—something Grandma left for me and me alone. Maybe I'll tell him later. Maybe I won't.

Chapter Two

When we get back to the car, my brother and sister are already in the backseat. Paul's nose is nestled in a book and Gwen's eyes are closed as she bops her head, listening to music on her headphones.

Mom stands beside the car, tapping her foot, arms crossed and lips stretched in a tight line. "Everyone's already on their way to the restaurant," she says to Dad, her voice an angry staccato. Turning to me, she gives my wet skirt a disapproving glance. "Kate, get a towel from the trunk to sit on. I don't want you making a mess of the car. And get the mud off your shoes."

Dad throws Mom a look, and when I go around the back of the car to get the towel, she follows me. She tries to smile, but it doesn't come even close to reaching her eyes, and I can still see the irritation sparking from her bright green irises.

"This is hard for all of us, Kate. It will get easier as time goes on." She says the words like she's trying to convince herself that they're true.

I want to say, *Oh, yeah? Is that why you're such a wreck? It gets easier? That's why you don't hang out with me anymore, ask me about my day, or try to find out if I like any of the guys at school? Because it gets easier?* The fact is, I'm not buying it. When Grandma died, a big hole opened up in me, and, even though a year's passed, that hole hasn't gotten any smaller. It's clear that Mom's hasn't gotten any smaller, either. In fact, I think it's gotten bigger.

But I just try to smile back at her, my lips quivering with the attempt. I try to make the *right* thing come out, something simple like, "Yeah, Mom, I know. I'll be fine." But the words get stuck in my throat. She turns on her heel and heads for the passenger seat. I stare at the back of her head, wishing I could have my old mom back.

As we drive to the restaurant, Dad tries to strike up conversation to relieve the uncomfortable silence, but Gwen's listening to her music, Paul's absorbed in his book, and Mom and I both look out of our windows, barely responding. Finally, Dad turns the radio up and settles for humming along. Relieved, I press back into my seat, discreetly patting my pocket to reassure myself that the bead is still there.

Before long, we're on Main Street in the tiny little town of Danville. I look around without interest, barely noticing the old buildings that line the street. We park behind an old-fashioned black and white police car, bearing the restaurant's name, "Mayberry Café," on its side. Dad lets out a laugh and explains that this restaurant is a throwback to some television show from the 1960s that featured a goofy police officer.

None of it really matters to me. All I know is that the bead is warm in my pocket as we climb out of the car and walk into the restaurant. Dad holds the door and breathes in deeply. "Mmmmm, smells like fried chicken," he says, patting his stomach with a smile.

The rest of the family remains quiet as we head up the stairs to our reserved room. I sit next to Evelyn, of course.

"Hey," she says, giving me a small smile.

"Hey," I respond, and stick my hand in my pocket to feel the bead, feeling guilty that I'm not in a rush to tell even her about it. I tell Evelyn *everything*, but I'm just not ready to talk about this. What would I say? How would I tell her? Would she think I'm crazy? Maybe it's just a coincidence, and I'm all worked up over nothing. Maybe somebody else had a bead with the letters K M R on it, and they lost it walking around those woods.

Right. Who am I trying to kid?

I feel sorry for the waitress as she approaches, looking nervous. I guess our crew would make *me* sweat if I were a waitress. There are nearly thirty in our party, with a bunch of kids, and most of us have red, puffy eyes from crying. I order a Coke and bury my head in the menu, as if I might actually order something other than a cheeseburger and fries. Really, I just don't feel like talking, not even to Evelyn. The other kids around me have finished with their menus, and they begin to talk among themselves. I wish that they would all just melt away so I could be alone.

My discomfort makes the time drag by, and it seems like forever before the waitress brings the drinks and takes our orders. When she leaves, I look around at the familiar faces sitting near me. As usual, I'm stuck at one of the kids' tables. Evelyn's eighteen-year-old brother, Dylan, is sitting across from me, and their little sister Ava is to his right. My sister Gwen is next to Ava—they're both thirteen, and best friends like me and Evelyn. Aunt Mary Ellen's oldest, fourteen-year-old Thomas, is on Dylan's left, and his twelve-year-old brother, Isaac, is next to him. Isaac idolizes Dylan, so he's straining around Thomas, hanging on to Dylan's every word. The two ten year olds—my brother Paul, and Mary Ellen's fourth child, Daniel—are at the far end of the table, while

Mary Ellen's youngest, Maria, is sitting on my right, busy coloring her paper place mat.

All of the other kids seem to have recovered from the awkwardness of being at the crash site, and I'm the only one who's not involved in a conversation. I still feel a little shaky, ready to cry at the drop of a hat, and I'm afraid to say anything to Evelyn, because I know that she'll see right through me and ask what's going on. So I mumble something about drying my skirt in the bathroom, scrape back my chair, and head down the stairs, hoping for a little privacy.

I find the bathroom, lock the door, and brace my hands on the edges of the sink, looking at myself in the mirror as if my reflection might hold some answers. What drew me to those trees? How did I find a tiny bead in the midst of that huge field, when the investigators missed it? Is it just a coincidence that it's *my bead*, or is it more than that? Is Grandma trying to speak to me somehow? And if she is, what is she saying?

The mirror holds no answers, so I turn to the hand dryer. It won't stay on unless I hold the button, and I find myself pressing it down with my left hand behind my back, while sticking my backside out toward the dryer, using my right hand to lift the skirt toward the air flow. Thank God, it's a one-person bathroom so there's no chance of someone walking in on me.

Five minutes later, finally satisfied with the results, I wash my hands and splash some water on my face before heading out of the bathroom. The walk back to our room takes me through a small gift shop. Not ready to face the crowd upstairs, I pretend to browse the collection of t-shirts, coffee mugs, and knickknacks. I put my hand in my pocket to reassure myself that the bead is still there, then draw it out, rolling it pensively within my fingers. I walk to the window to seek the sun's light, where I use my fingernail to scrape the dirt from the engraved letter K.

Absorbed in the bead, I don't even realize that someone else has come into the gift shop area until I hear a discreet cough. Looking up, I see a girl standing only a few feet away and hastily shove the bead back into my pocket. She watches me with interest, and tucks an unruly strand of hair behind her ear.

"Can I help you?" she asks, after a too-long pause. The girl looks like she's about eighteen, with blond hair that's pulled back into a messy ponytail. She wears the restaurant's uniform of black pants and a maroon shirt bearing the restaurant's logo.

"Um, no. I was just looking."

"Okay. Well, my name's Chelsea, if you need anything." She shrugs, starting to walk away, but then pauses to ask, "You here with that big group upstairs?"

"Yeah, that's my family."

Her eyes get big. "Wow, that's a big family! Do you guys get together like that often?"

"Well, we used to. I mean, we do Christmas and Thanksgiving and Easter and stuff, but . . . this . . ." I swallow and blink my eyes, not wanting to cry in front of someone I don't even know. "This is different."

"Oh, like somebody's big birthday, or something?"

A small, bitter laugh escapes me. "No, not a birthday. My grandma was on that plane a year ago. The one that . . ." The words catch in my throat.

Chelsea's hand flies to her mouth. Her bright eyes widen and fill with pity. "Oh my gosh. I'm so sorry. How awful!"

"Yeah, well . . . it takes time, but you get over it," I lie with a shrug.

She tries to change the subject. "Uh, so, do you . . . live near here?"

"About forty-five minutes away, in Indy. It's the first time we've been out here."

"That's cool. I mean, well, it's not, but . . ."

I decide to take pity on her. "This is a nice store you've got here," I motion around me.

"Seriously?" she rolls her eyes. "Yeah, I guess—if you're into washed-up, old television shows." She laughs, and then looks around a bit nervously. "Well, like I said, if you need anything, just ask." She starts to walk toward the counter, but stops and turns around.

"Hey, can I ask you something?"

"I guess so," I say, but I'm pretty sure I'm not going to want to answer.

"The thing you were looking at when I first came in, that you had in your hand. What was that?"

I put my fingers in my pocket and wrap them around the bead, which is warm from being tucked safely in my pocket. Without even thinking about it, I pull the bead out and hold it in my palm for her to see. I don't understand why I would talk about it with this stranger, when I haven't even told Evelyn, or my dad, but suddenly the words are tumbling from my lips.

"It's a rosary bead. You know, like from a rosary that old ladies pray with? My grandmother had a special one that my grandfather had made for her; it had a bead engraved with the initials of each of her children. Then, when they grew up and got married, she had beads made for their spouses. And when they had kids, she added beads for the kids. So we each had our own bead, and it had our initials engraved on it. She said she prayed for us every day."

"Wow. She sounds like a really special grandmother," Chelsea says.

I pause, and then say quietly, "I found this out in the field today, during the memorial service. This is *my* bead." I continue to stare at the silver bead in my hand for a moment, then finally look up. Chelsea's face has gone white, and she's staring at the bead, too. I wouldn't have thought it possible, but those big brown eyes have gotten even wider than before.

After what seems like forever, she shifts her gaze to mine. Her mouth is hanging open, and her jaw moves, like she wants to say something but can't find the words. She reaches her hand out and grasps hold of the nearby counter, as if to prevent her legs from going out from under her.

Finally, still looking straight into my eyes, she breathes, "I found a bead, just like that one. Only it said E M L. I gave it to my friend, Emma." She looks back down at the bead in my palm. "Emma Marie Lowry. E M L. She—" Her shocked eyes find mine again. "She thinks it saved her life."

Chapter Three

We stand there, staring at each other for a long time. Then, I drag my eyes away, desperately looking for a place to sit down. The window sill is narrow, but big enough to offer some support, and I shakily fall back against it, pressing my fisted hand, with the bead inside, against my stomach.

At that moment, I hear footsteps descending the stairs to the left of the shop. I jump to attention as Mom rounds the corner and stops abruptly.

"Kate! There you are. We've got our food and yours is getting—" Mom breaks off when she realizes that both Chelsea and I are gaping at her. "Kate, what's going on? What are you doing?" she demands.

"Nothing! I was just, um, looking around the gift shop," I reply, trying to sound normal. I look desperately around the shop, trying to find a reason to stay for a few more minutes. "Um, I was just asking about these . . . these coffee mugs. I'll . . . I'll be right up, okay?"

Mom's lips purse and her jaw sets. "Kate, this is an important time, and I don't think it's appropriate for you to be hanging out in the gift shop instead of being with your family. Come and eat."

How can I argue? She's right. It's not appropriate. So I shoot a glance at Chelsea and follow Mom back upstairs.

The room is relatively quiet, as everyone is busy eating. Evelyn casts a glance at me, then goes back to eating, and I can tell that she's a little miffed that I took off. I look at the cheeseburger and fries on my plate, but my appetite is long gone. Instead, I grab my Coke and suck on the straw, trying to think of what I should say to Evelyn. I come up blank and settle for a whispered, "I'm sorry. I'll explain later." Then I set the cup down and take a bite of my now-cold burger.

Keeping my eyes on my plate to avoid meeting the gaze of anyone else at the table, I think over what Chelsea just told me. E M L. That would be Aunt Liz's bead. E, for Elizabeth. And this girl Emma thinks the bead saved her life? How could that be? Lots of questions flood my thoughts. Where did Chelsea find the bead? How long ago did she find it? Isn't all this way too big a coincidence to actually *be* a coincidence? I desperately want to abandon my plate and my family, and march back down to the gift shop to find out everything I can about the bead, Emma, and how it could have saved her life, but I feel Mom's eyes on me. Giving her a guilty glance, it's obvious that she's more than a little ticked that I disappeared for so long.

I try to make small talk with Evelyn, suddenly wanting nothing more than to tell her everything that's happened in the last hour: being drawn to that spot in the trees while everybody was praying the Rosary, finding the bead—with *my initials* on it—then learning that someone else has another bead, and thinks that *it saved her life*. But there's no way I can talk about that here, not with the whole family around. Who knows how they'd react? I don't even know what's really going on. So I ask Evelyn how she did on the algebra test Thursday, and how she's coming along on her biology project, and when her first softball game is. I talk to five-year-old Maria on my left, oohing and aahing over the picture she's colored on her place mat, and make a feeble effort to pretend that everything is normal and okay.

The time drags on, and on, and on. I can't help casting an occasional glance toward the stairway, wishing that I could find an excuse to go back down there and learn the rest of the story. Finally, I see Chelsea standing at the top of the stairs with her purse over her shoulder, car keys in hand. She gives me a helpless look, and a quick wave. She's leaving, and that's it. My chance to get answers to all my questions is lost.

Back at home the next morning, we go to ten o'clock Mass with the rest of the family. It almost feels like old times, when we would meet for Mass, filling up four rows of pews, with Grandma and Papa at the center. Afterward, though, instead of heading to Grandma and Papa's house, like we used to, we go down the street to Evelyn's house for brunch. Aunt Susan has put together a huge spread of quiche, roast beef, cinnamon rolls, and more.

I had hoped to finally get a chance to talk to Evelyn about the bead, but the house is packed with relatives, and getting a moment alone proves next to impossible. It's raining, so we can't go outside. Gwen and Ava are in the girls' bedroom; the boys are playing video games in the basement; and every other space in the house seems to be crawling with little kids, adults, or both.

At one thirty, Mom tells me it's time to go. I ask if I can stick around, hoping to be able to talk to Evelyn after everyone else leaves, but Mom insists that she needs me to watch Paul while she and Dad take Gwen to softball practice and go shopping. I roll my eyes but head to the car.

At least my "babysitting" job is easy. Paul sits on the couch the whole time watching baseball, while I read *Lord of the Flies* for English class. The moment Mom, Dad, and Gwen walk in the door, I ask if I can go to Evelyn's house. Mom's lips stretch in a tight line. *Seriously? Why is she mad at me now?* Fortunately, Dad nods his assent before reminding me to be home for dinner. I rush upstairs to my room and call Evelyn.

"Ev, it's me. Can I come over? I've gotta talk to you."

"Yeah, sure. What's up?"

"I can't say right now, but I'll fill you in when I get there. Something happened yesterday. Something really weird. And cool. And—well—I want to tell you about it and see what you think."

I hang up and throw on my green puffer jacket, gloves, and hat as I run for the back door, rushing to grab my bike out of the garage. I pop my ear buds in, hit play, and jump on my bike.

It's an easy ride to Evelyn's house, only seven blocks. Fortunately, the sun has come out and warmed the day significantly, and I find I'm actually hot in my winter gear. My feet slow on the pedals as I get closer to the house, and by the time I arrive and set the kickstand, I'm filled with anxiety. This whole thing is weird. What if Evelyn thinks I'm crazy? I take a deep breath, willing the butterflies in my stomach to settle down. Why on earth am I so nervous to tell her what happened?

After a few seconds, I approach the back door and give it a quick rap, before peering inside to look in the kitchen. No one's in there, so I walk on in and call out Evelyn's name. Hearing her response, I head up the stairs toward her room. She's nestled against the pillows of the bed with a book propped on raised knees. She looks up as I walk into the room.

"Hey. What's up?" She asks, as she pushes from the pillows and pulls her legs in to sit cross-legged on the blue-and-green-striped comforter.

I pull out her desk chair and plop down, chewing at my lip as I wonder where to start. I look over Evelyn's head and see the crucifix that hangs above her bed. I don't pray often, but I find myself offering a silent prayer that she'll believe me—and that she'll know what we should do. Then I take a deep breath and begin.

"You remember Grandma's rosary? The one with everybody's initials carved into the silver beads?"

"Yeah, Dad said that she prayed at least one Rosary every day for us," Evelyn answers.

I extend my legs so that I can reach into my pocket. Drawing my hand out, I unfurl my palm wordlessly, watching her face as recognition washes over it.

Evelyn stares at the bead for a long time, speechless, before carefully reaching into my palm and taking it into her own fingers. She looks at the engraved letters, running her forefinger over them as I have done so many times in the last twenty-four hours. Finally, she looks me in the eye and expels, almost in a whisper, "Wh . . . where did you find this?"

I tell her the whole story, about skipping out on the Rosary yesterday when we were in the field, and walking to the trees, and how I felt so *drawn* to those trees, but didn't know why. I tell her about finding the bead, and crying, Dad coming and taking me to the car, and then going to the restaurant and meeting Chelsea. I tell her about E M L— Emma—who now has Aunt Liz's bead.

"But here's the crazy thing, Ev. This girl, *Emma*? She thinks the bead saved her life!"

"No way!" Evelyn's been listening without moving. Now she leans toward me, clearly intrigued. "Saved her life? How? What happened?"

"That's the problem; I don't know! Mom walked in at that very moment and made me come back to the table. I wanted to go back and talk to this Chelsea girl more, but I knew Mom would kill me. Then, before we were finished with lunch, Chelsea came upstairs, waved goodbye, and took off!"

"We have to find out!" Evelyn exclaims. "We've got to know what happened! And Aunt Liz should have her bead! It was Grandma's, and *she* should have it!"

"I know, I know! But what can I do? It's not like I can ride my bike all the way out there and talk to Chelsea, let alone get the bead back from her friend. And what if this Emma won't give it back? What then?"

"Well, duh. For starters, you can call the restaurant and ask for Chelsea. If she's not there, you ask when she's working next, and you call back then. Come on, Kate! Where's your brain?"

I squirm a little at her criticism. Okay, that *is* pretty obvious. I don't know why I hadn't thought of it before.

"You're right," I answer. "We just have to get the phone number for the restaurant."

Now, if I were a normal sixteen-year-old, I'd pull my smartphone out of my pocket and look up Mayberry Café. Unfortunately, my mom is the wicked witch of cell phones, and won't let me have one. She's in cahoots with Evelyn's mom—and most of the family, for that matter—so Ev doesn't have one, either.

"Let's go look it up on the computer in the kitchen," Evelyn suggests.

"Wait," I say. "I think we should keep this a secret for now. I don't know why, I just . . . do. Okay?"

"Sure," Evelyn nods. "I get it. We'll see if anyone's in the kitchen. If the coast is clear, we'll look up the number. If not, we'll figure something else out."

We stroll into the kitchen, pretending that we're hungry and looking for a snack. Of course, Aunt Susan's already in there, chopping vegetables for dinner. The family computer is on the planning desk in a corner of the kitchen, in full view of the sink where Aunt Susan is standing. She'll definitely wonder what we're up to if we sit down and google the number for the restaurant. We each grab a banana and head back upstairs to regroup.

"What do we do now?" Evelyn asks once we're out of earshot.

"I don't know. We can't do it at my house either. The computer's right there in the living room, and *somebody* will be in there watching TV." I tap my finger on my lips.

Evelyn's face screws up in a grimace. "We could ask Dylan if we can use his phone," she says in a whisper.

I nod my agreement, and we head down the hallway to Dylan's room. Evelyn raps on the closed door, but there's no answer. She puts her ear to the wooden surface, and I do the same. We can hear Dylan's voice on the other side, and from the syrupy sound of it, it's pretty obvious he's talking to his girlfriend.

Evelyn rolls her eyes and whispers, "Ugh! He could be on the phone for *hours!*"

We head back to Evelyn's room, and plop down into our seats, each of us thinking quietly. Evelyn chews on her lip and I gnaw on a snag in my pinkie nail. How can we get a phone number without being detected by any of our family members?

Finally, I pipe up. "What about the library?"

"Brilliant!" Evelyn jumps off the bed. "Let's go!"

We're out the door and in her garage before it occurs to us that we need to let our parents know where we're going.

We run into the house. Evelyn stops in the kitchen to tell her mom, while I call my dad. Then we both hop on our bikes and race down the driveway.

The library on a Sunday afternoon is dead. Finding a computer is no problem, and we quickly do a search to find the phone number for the café. We jot the number down and head right back out the door. We're nearly at our bikes when Evelyn stops suddenly.

"Wait. Our parents are going to wonder why we went to the library and came back empty handed. Do you think maybe we should check out some books?"

"Shoot!" I stomp my foot and punch a fist at the air. "But what if Chelsea's working right now? What if we take too long, and miss her?"

But we both know that we can't come home from a trip to the library without a single book, and without further discussion, Evelyn grabs my sleeve and pulls me back into the building.

Fifteen minutes later, fines paid and books in hand, Evelyn and I are back on our bikes. Of course, neither of us thought to bring a backpack, and we struggle to steer one handed. We hurry as much as we can, and nearly collide into each other going through the back door.

Evelyn's mom is still at the kitchen sink, and looks up as we come rushing in. "Wow, girls! What's got you in such a hurry?"

Evelyn slows down abruptly. "Oh, nothing, Mom! We just want to look at our books!" She answers, without actually looking at her mom.

Fortunately, we're both pretty bookish, so Aunt Susan just raises an eyebrow, smiles, and says, "Alright, girls. Have fun."

Evelyn grabs two bottles of water from the fridge, and we head upstairs. Once we're safely in her room, I sit down on the bed and stare at the phone, my heart racing.

"Oh, come on, Kate! You've just gotta *do* it!" Evelyn grabs the cordless phone and holds her hand out, wordlessly demanding the paper that has the number scratched across it.

I take a deep breath and reach into my pocket, my fingers colliding with the bead as I fish for the small slip of paper. I hand it to Evelyn. She dials the number, and then hands the phone to me.

The phone rings several times before someone answers.

"Um, hi. Uh, is Ch . . . Chelsea working right now?" I stammer.

"Her shift just ended." The feminine voice on the other end says. My heart plummets. "But, hang on. She might still be here. Can I tell her who's calling?"

"Um, well, my name is Kate Roberts. I talked to her in the gift shop yesterday."

"Ohhhh, she told me about you! Just a minute, let me check and see if she's still here." The line goes silent as the girl puts me on hold. I look at Evelyn, startled that Chelsea might have told this stranger the story when I haven't even told anyone but Evelyn yet.

"Hello?"

I recognize the voice instantly, and jump off the bed in excitement. Evelyn jumps up too, and puts her head next to mine so that she can hear the conversation.

"Hi. Chelsea?"

"Yeah, hi! Kate, right?"

I mumble an affirmation.

"I was hoping you'd call. I had no idea how to get a hold of you. I talked to my friend Emma, and told her all about your bead. She really wants to meet you and tell you her story. Do you think it would be possible to do that?"

Evelyn jerks her head away excitedly. She's nearly jumping up and down, mouthing, "Yes! Yes! Yes!"

I have no idea how I'm going to get all the way out to Danville, but I guess we'll figure something out.

"Um, sure. I can do that. When?"

"Well, how about Thursday?"

I look at Ev, but she's shaking her head. "Tomorrow!" she mouths.

"Uh, Thursday won't work. Could we do it tomorrow?" I ask.

"I'll have to check with Emma, but, yeah, that will probably work."

I give Chelsea Evelyn's phone number and hang up. Then, it sinks in. I've just made plans to meet someone, nearly an hour away, on a school day, with no transportation to or from the meeting. My parents don't know that I'm doing this, Evelyn's parents don't know, *nobody* with a car knows about this! And I hadn't really been planning to tell anyone about it, either! At least, not yet!

I turn on Evelyn. "Tomorrow? Tomorrow! Why tomorrow? What have we just done? How on *earth* are we going to get all the way out there *tomorrow*?!!"

"Kate! Relax! Aunt Liz! She's still in town, staying with Uncle Jon and Aunt Kathy! We just have to tell *her*. She's cool, and *it's her bead*. She'll take us. But she leaves on Tuesday, so it *has* to be tomorrow."

I look at the clock. It's almost five, and I'll have to go home for dinner soon. We don't have much time.

"Okay. You've got a point. Do you have her number?"

"Uh, no." Evelyn cringes. "But I'm sure my mom does! We just have to find her phone, look in the contacts, and *voilà!*"

For the record, I'm no angel. But I'm not altogether comfortable with snooping around someone else's phone. I think about it briefly before writing it off as Evelyn's responsibility. It's her mom, her snooping. I'm just a bystander.

"Okay. Go for it. I'll wait here." I sit back down on the bed and open my new library book.

Evelyn shoots me an exasperated look before tiptoeing from the room. Five minutes later, she's back, phone in hand, but she doesn't look happy.

"It's dead," she whispers.

"Where's the charger?"

"I don't know! I looked, and I can't find it!"

"Well, what about your dad's phone? Aunt Liz is *his* sister. He'll have her number."

"You're right, but his phone is where it always is. In his pocket."

"Shoot! Okay, we'll just have to find the charger."

Somehow, my I'm-just-a-bystander resolution flies out the window and I'm now involved in a full-scale hunt for a cell phone charger. We look in the car, Aunt Susan's purse, and the office. Not there. Finally, twenty minutes later, we're standing in her parents' bedroom, and Evelyn whispers in desperation, "Saint Anthony, Saint Anthony, won't you please come around? Mom's charger is lost, and must be found."

I chuckle. As if! I've always thought that was the dumbest thing—praying to a saint to help you find something you've lost!

Evelyn suddenly drops to her knees, picks up the bed skirt, and peers under the bed. "Ha! There it is!" Grabbing a hanger, she swipes under the bed, and sure enough, there's the charger.

Evelyn's smile is huge and her eyes sparkle. She looks up at the ceiling. "Thank you, Saint Anthony! You rock!"

I'm speechless. I seriously didn't think Evelyn bought into that stuff. It is *just* a coincidence! Rolling my eyes, I turn on my heel and leave the room, breathing a sigh of relief once we're safely back in Evelyn's room.

We plug in her mom's phone and wait impatiently while it gains enough charge to power on. Finally, Evelyn locates Aunt Liz's contact info, and holds the phone out so I can see the number. Once again, I'm nervous to pick up the phone, and stare at the cordless handset like it's a slimy, stinky fish. Evelyn—ever the courageous one—grabs it from her bed-side table and presses in the numbers.

I can hear the phone ringing on the other end from where I stand, but Aunt Liz doesn't pick up. Evelyn leaves a vague message, asking Aunt Liz to call her, and hangs up. Then we both sit there willing the phone to ring. No such luck.

Thirty minutes later, it's time for me to go home and we still haven't heard from Aunt Liz. We did, however, hear back from Chelsea, and we're all set to meet her and Emma at the restaurant tomorrow afternoon. Now, we just have to find a ride.

I have a sick feeling in the pit of my stomach as I pedal away from Evelyn's house. We've got to make this work. I really need to know what happened to this Emma person, and how the bead saved her life. I realize that getting that information is suddenly more important to me than just about anything else.

When I walk in the door of my house, I quickly recognize the smell of a frozen pizza cooking. *Not again*, I think. My mom used to love cooking, but lately we've been eating an awful lot of stuff that comes from the freezer or a box.

I suffer through dinner, glancing at my watch every few minutes. Dad tries to keep some conversation going, but it's an uphill battle. Mom stares at her plate without saying a word, chewing mechanically. Paul's clearly anxious to go outside and join the neighbor kids' baseball game, Gwen wants to read her book, and I want to call Evelyn.

I dutifully help clean the dishes before grabbing the cordless phone and running up to my room, where I dial Evelyn's number.

"Have you heard from Aunt Liz yet?" I ask, without even saying hello.

"Nope," she answers, her voice laced with concern. "Do you think I should call her again?"

"No! If you do, she'll wonder what's so important, and probably mention it to Uncle Jon and Aunt Kathy. They'll end up calling your mom, and then everybody's going to be asking all sorts of questions."

"Kate, let me ask you this: Just *why* is it so important that we keep this a secret?"

"I don't know! I just feel like we have to. You know how Mom's been ever since Grandma died. She's really down, doesn't get excited or happy about *anything*, and it's like she's just looking for a reason to say 'no' to me. I guess I'm afraid that if she finds out, she'll tell me that it's all nonsense, and that I'm wasting my time even looking into it. She's really bitter about the whole 'God thing' lately, anyways."

I pause in front of my window, looking out at the gathering darkness. "You know what I heard her tell my dad a while back? She was talking about how Grandma used to go to Mass every day, and how she prayed *all the time*. And then she said, 'Look where it got her. What a waste!' Who knows what she'd say if I told her about all of this!"

For the record, my parents have never been very religious, and I don't think my dad believes in God at all. Sure, we used to go to Mass every Sunday, and they send us to Catholic schools, but we don't pray or talk about religion outside of that. It's like we're just going through the motions, because that's what we're *supposed* to do. Nonetheless, Mom's words really surprised me, especially since Grandma was obviously so into her faith.

I swallow hard and continue, "I know it doesn't make any sense, but I guess I'm worried about what Mom will do if this whole thing turns out to be some kind of miracle, or if we find out it's all a bunch of junk. I'm afraid she'll get upset either way, and she's *already* upset. All the time. I don't want her to lose whatever faith she has left."

I stop as my own words sink in. I hadn't really thought it all the way through before, so it's like I'm hearing my own thoughts for the first time.

"So I guess that's why I want to keep it a secret," I finish lamely.

The line is silent. I begin to wonder if Evelyn is still there. Then, finally, "Okay. I get it. We'll keep it a secret. But we've got to have a plan B, in case Aunt Liz doesn't call."

"Do the city buses run out there?"

"I don't think so."

"A taxi?" I suggest hopefully.

"Do you have any idea how much that would cost?"

"Yeah, both of our allowances combined for the next six months."

"Right."

Silence. I chew on my lip, searching for an idea.

Finally, Evelyn says in a slightly choked voice, "Dylan?"

Well, there *is* Dylan. He's got his own car, an old Honda Accord, which he constantly pushes to the very limits of its speedometer. If these beads really have some kind of power, and I take mine with me, we might just survive the trip out to Danville and back.

I take a deep breath. "Dylan." Mustering up my courage, I agree. "Okay. Go ask him and call me back."

Evelyn hangs up the phone, and I sit down to work on my homework. I can't seem to focus, though, and my mind wanders to thinking about how our family has changed since Grandma died.

We used to be one of those families that got together every weekend. Grandma and Papa had the coolest house, and there was no place we'd rather be. Papa would always say, "Well, that's why we built this place. We wanted a grand-kid magnet." He'd smile, look around at all of us, and say, "I guess it worked."

Yeah, it did. The pool, the games, the giant TV . . . there was always something to do at Grandma and Papa's house. But it was more than just the house. It was the people inside, people who always welcomed us with a smile and the unspoken assurance that we were wanted and loved.

Grandma and Papa had seven kids. Well, that's how I always think of it, but Grandma would have told you that she had eleven—seven that God gave her as gifts on earth and four that he needed up in heaven. I never understood how she could be so accepting of having lost four babies, but I guess that was just Grandma.

Those seven kids used to be super close, and six of them still live in town, within twenty minutes of each other. Evelyn's dad, Uncle David, is the oldest of the kids. He and Aunt Susan have three children. My mom's next, and we have three kids in our family, too. Then comes Aunt Mary Ellen, who's only a year younger than my mom. Apparently the two of them were like twins growing up because they were so close in age, but they've grown apart in the last few years, especially since Grandma died. Mom doesn't talk about it, but I think they don't have much in common anymore. Aunt Mary Ellen is more like Grandma. She and her husband Robert have five kids so far, and who knows how many more they'll have down the road.

After Mary Ellen is Uncle Matthew. He and his wife, Aunt Janey, have five kids, too. Then there's Uncle Joseph, the priest. There was another brother after Joseph—Mark—but he died shortly after he was born. Uncle Jonathan is next, and he and Aunt Kathy don't have any kids, even though they've been married awhile. Grandma's three miscarriages came in between Uncle Jon and Aunt Liz, which means that Aunt Liz is a lot younger than everyone else. I always thought she had to be a bit lonely, or maybe a bit spoiled, or both. Regardless, she's a journalist in Denver and she's super cool. Since Evelyn and I are the oldest girls, she sometimes takes us out for movies, manicures, and things like that when she's in town.

So, seven kids, sixteen grandkids, and now both Grandma and Papa are gone. When we're together it seems like everybody's still pretty close, but we almost never get *everyone* together anymore. We've all got our own activities, and our own friends, and our own lives. No one has a house big enough for everyone, anyways. I guess Grandma and Papa were the glue holding us together, and without them, we all seem to be drifting apart.

The phone rings, breaking through my reverie. I grab it before anyone else in the family can, figuring it's Evelyn.

"He'll do it," she says, as soon as I answer.

I let out the breath I hadn't realized I was holding.

29

"But we have to pay for the gas."

Okay, that's doable.

"And I have to do his chores for a week to make up for his time."

Better Evelyn than me.

"So, what's the story for our parents?" she asks.

Oh, tough one. I've never snuck around like this before, and even though my mom's been driving me a bit nuts lately, I really don't want to lie to her. But, I see no alternative.

"How about shopping?" I reply, reluctantly.

"Yeah, I guess that would work. I don't really want to lie to my parents, though." Evelyn echoes my concerns.

"You can go to confession on Saturday." I try to be flippant. "Anyways, it'll sort of be true. We can buy something at the gift shop."

"Good one. How about you come to my house after school. Dylan's got a meeting with the guidance counselor, but he can take us after that."

And so our plans are set. I hang up and attempt to read my history book again. It's going to be a long night.

Chapter Four

Well, I didn't sleep well at all last night, and I probably failed my history test today. But all I really care about right now is that Evelyn and I are walking toward her house, and in less than two hours we'll be meeting Chelsea and her friend, Emma.

We say hello to Aunt Susan, grab a snack, and head up to Evelyn's room to do our homework. Evelyn's favorite color is blue, and the light blue hue of her walls, blue-and-green-striped comforter and green pillows provide a soothing backdrop for us to chill out and wait. She sits at her desk, while I sprawl on the bed, *Lord of the Flies* open in front of me. Evelyn plugs her speakers in, and plays her "homework" mix.

Evelyn may be my best friend, but we definitely don't share the same taste in music. The first song in the playlist is a Gregorian chant—a bunch of monks singing in Latin. The second features some famous children's choir, singing another hymn, again in a foreign language. I don't understand why anyone would want to listen to music they can't understand, but Evelyn listens to this all the time. She's tried to explain it, saying that the songs remind her of angels singing and put her in a "celestial state of mind"—whatever that means. Personally, I'd rather listen to the latest Top 40.

My mind wanders as I think about Evelyn's comment about singing angels. Like I told her last night, I'm not really

31

into the whole "religion" thing, even though I go to a Catholic school. But I do *believe* there's a God. People, animals, the earth . . . it's all way too complicated to be just a coincidence. There has to be some sort of "higher being" that made it all come together so nicely. And Jesus? Well, he seems like a pretty cool dude, so I guess I don't have a problem with him, either.

We learned about purgatory in religion class, so I guess most people don't go straight to heaven. Mrs. Dawson had us look up lots of quotes in the Bible, like when Jesus said, "the gate is narrow but the path is wide," or, "be perfect, even as my Father in heaven is perfect." And Saint Paul said something about being tested through fire. Once we learned about it, purgatory made a lot of sense to me. I mean, everybody's always talking about heaven, but I can see how most of us aren't really good enough on earth to get a direct ticket to paradise.

When we talked about purgatory, Mrs. Dawson was *all over* the fact that a person who goes to heaven is a saint, not an angel. Something about angels being celestial beings or spirits, so people can't just "become" angels.

As I listen to the music, I think about Grandma as a saint, not an angel, and I hope that she's up in heaven. Is she watching over us? Can she go to God and ask him for special favors? Is *she* somehow behind me finding the rosary bead?

I wore the bead to school today, on a long silver chain I found in my jewelry box. It's tucked safely into my shirt, where no one can see it. Every so often, it shifts against my skin and I remember that it's there. Somehow, I feel peaceful whenever I think about it. Now, as I lie on Evelyn's bed, I take it out and run my fingers over it.

I force my attention back to my book—we've got a test on it tomorrow—and I read most of the final chapter before I hear the sound of Dylan's voice downstairs. Finally. Evelyn and I both jump up and, realizing that we're still in our uniforms, quickly change. Evelyn puts on a pair of blue leggings and a blue-and-green-striped shirt. I snicker as I realize that she matches her room, but I don't say anything. I put on jeans and a long-sleeved Knights t-shirt, showing my school spirit.

We try to be all nonchalant when we go downstairs to wait for Dylan. Evelyn tells her mom that Dylan's agreed to take us shopping. I stare at the back door, uncomfortable with the distortion of the truth.

Dylan's not in as big a hurry as we are, and seems to take forever to get changed and ready to go. Ten minutes later, we're finally in the car, headed toward Chelsea, Emma, and another bead.

It's a beautiful day outside, with just a hint of a chill, as if winter is trying to pull the spring back into its grasp. The trees are beginning to show hints of green, and a few cro- cuses have popped up in the landscaping of the homes. As Dylan speeds away from the house, I try to focus on the scenery rather than the speedometer, grasping the door handle as he rounds a corner too quickly.

Once we're out of the city traffic, Dylan looks at me in the rearview mirror. "So, Kate, Evelyn told me a little bit about what's going on, but I'd like to hear it from you," he says in his most authoritative eighteen-year-old voice.

I take a deep breath and begin to tell him the story, just as I told it to Evelyn yesterday afternoon.

"So now we're going to find out what happened to Emma, and hopefully we'll be able to get Aunt Liz's bead back, too." I finish, as we sit at yet another stoplight on the road to Danville.

Dylan doesn't comment, but instead turns up the radio, seeming lost in thought. Finally, when he glides smoothly into a parking spot, he remarks, "Well, let's go find out what the rest of the story is," and climbs out of the car.

The door chimes as we enter the restaurant. Chelsea's sitting at a booth just past the gift shop, and a slender girl with short, brown, spiky hair sits next to her. Evelyn and I slide into the other side of the booth, while Dylan pulls a chair up to the end of the table.

I introduce my cousins, and Chelsea introduces her friend, Emma, before asking if she can get each of us a soda. As she heads for the kitchen to get our drinks, I turn to the other girl. She looks like she's a bit older than Chelsea, probably nineteen or so. She has a very confident air, with a warm and friendly gleam in her eyes.

"So, I guess you came about this," Emma says as she pulls a necklace out from under her shirt, revealing the bead that dangles from it. A little bit reluctantly, she unfastens the necklace and places it in the palm of her hand. As she begins talking, she continues to look at the bead.

"Chelsea was leaving work one day last summer. As she looked for her keys, something fell out of her purse. When she went to pick it up, she found *this* in a crack of the side-walk. She picked it up and saw that it had my initials on it. We're kind of like sisters—I've been living with her family since my mom had to move away for her job two years ago, and I didn't want to leave our school in the middle of the year. She was so excited when she got home that day and showed me this bead! I thought it was pretty cool, too, but always felt a little guilty keeping it because I knew it belonged to someone else. Of course, I didn't know who to give it back to, so . . . Anyway, I put the bead on this chain, and wore it every day. There was something about wearing it that . . . I don't know. Something about it just made me feel good."

Emma looks up from the bead in her palm, and glances between me, Dylan, and Evelyn before settling her gaze back on me. "Then one day I was driving to work early in the morning—I work at the grocery store in town. A car suddenly came hurtling toward me, on the wrong side of the road. We found out later it was a drunk driver. The car slammed into mine, and flipped mine over. I don't really remember that, or hanging upside down in my seat waiting for the ambulance to come—like I've blocked it out. But there's one thing I do remember. I was really scared, and couldn't stop thinking that I was going to die. Then the weirdest thing happened."

Emma shakes her head, as if she hardly believes it herself, "I smelled *roses*," she looks across the table at me and Evelyn. "There was no mistaking it. It was December, but I definitely smelled roses. Then, I heard a woman's voice, and suddenly I knew—" her voice chokes off, and her expression changes to one of wonder, "I just knew that everything would be okay. The woman told me to hang on, and that I was going to be okay. I felt her take my hand and it comforted me." Emma holds her right hand in the palm of her left, and stares at it as she remembers. "People told me that they had to pry the car door open with the Jaws of Life, and the paramedics said that I shouldn't have survived. I was out cold when they first found me, but came to when they were pulling me from the car. I asked them afterward if they had seen the woman who was with me, and no one had. But you know what I had in my hand?" She holds up the bead on its chain. "This bead. I don't know how it got there. It had been around my neck. The chain wasn't even broken. But the bead was in my hand." She looks me straight in the eye as her own fill with tears, "And it smelled like roses."

Everyone is silent for several moments while we all soak it in, and I feel goose bumps on my arms and legs. Then, a little awkwardly, Emma finishes, "I know it seems crazy, but I feel like—somehow—this bead saved my life."

Now silence reigns for what seems like an eternity. What do you say to that? I'm sure not going to open my mouth and say something stupid.

Finally, Dylan picks up his Coke and slurps noisily at the remains. The spell is broken.

Emma removes the bead from its chain, and holds it out to me.

"No, I can't take it," I say. "It's yours now."

"No, it isn't. Chelsea told me that it was your grand-mother's. And she told me about how you found another one in the field where . . . I wouldn't feel right keeping it. Besides, it's served its purpose. I don't think I'll need it anymore." She places the bead in my palm, folds my fingers over it, and gently pushes my fisted hand toward me.

More silence. I feel tears well up in my eyes, and a single drop slides down my cheek. Beside me, I hear Evelyn sniffle.

Chelsea finally breaks the tension. "So, what are you going to do now? Will you try to find the rest of the beads?"

Chapter Five

I sit for a moment in stunned silence. The thought of searching for all the beads had never even crossed my mind. Evelyn
and I turn and look at each other, and our eyes widen with
excitement. Is it possible? Could we do it?

"But how . . ."

"Where would we—" Ev and I both start talking at the
same time, then collapse in nervous giggles, relieved by the
change of subject after the emotion of hearing Emma's story.

Dylan interrupts our laughter, rolling his eyes, and
scooting back from the table. "Come on, guys. We've gotta
go. And I'm not driving you out here again, so if you're going
to look for more beads you'll have to find another driver."

Evelyn doesn't budge from her seat. "Fine. We'll find
someone else," She crosses her arms with a look of defiance,
even toward the big brother she idolizes. "Anyways, we'll
both have our driver's licenses before the end of the
summer."

"We'll ride our bikes if we have to!" I say, crossing my
fingers behind my back in the hope that it won't come to
that.

"Chelsea and I would help," Emma says, and I breathe a
sigh of relief. "We could bring the beads to you, or even just
put them in the mail."

Chelsea chimes in, "Yeah, we'd definitely help. But first, we have to figure out how you're going to *find* more beads."

That's easy. I've helped advertise for our school plays, after all. "We'll put flyers up," I say with a shrug, "and we could even put ads in the newspaper."

Chelsea nods her head, "We'd post a flyer here at the restaurant!"

Emma agrees, "They'd put one up at the grocery store, too, and we could put them all along Main Street."

"It's settled then. We'll try to find the rest of the beads," I say.

Dylan's waiting impatiently, so I start to slide out of the booth, but then I stop and look back at Evelyn. "What if we could find them *all*? Do you think there could be other stories like Emma's?"

She raises her eyebrows and says resolutely, "Well, there's only one way to find out."

When we leave the café, Chelsea and Emma feel like old friends, even though we've just met, and they're older than we are. We exchange hugs and agree to be in touch soon. I've got both of their phone numbers and email addresses safely stashed in my pocket.

Evelyn and I are both giddy with excitement. As we drive home, Evelyn sits twisted around in her seat next to her brother, and I lean forward in mine, gripping her head-rest so we can talk more easily. Still awestruck by what we heard, we can't stop talking about Emma's story.

"Who do you think the voice was?" I ask.

"Well, duh! It was the Blessed Mother!" Evelyn responds.

"The Virgin Mary? No, way!" I object. "Maybe it was Grandma."

Unexpectedly, Dylan chimes in, "I'm with Evelyn. I've heard stories about people smelling roses when they've had mystical experiences. It was Mary."

I touch the two rosary beads now hanging on my chain. "So, you think Emma's bead has some sort of special link to the Mother of God?"

"I don't know about *power*, but there is something *special* about it," Evelyn answers.

"You know, she could have just been imagining things," Dylan, ever the skeptic, adds. "Maybe Emma knew on some subconscious level that the bead was from a rosary. Maybe that, along with being in a really scary accident, made her dream up the rose smell and the woman's voice."

I think a moment, then, "No. Ev's right. There's something special about these beads. My bead *drew me to it*. This bead *saved someone's life*. There's something going on here, and the only way we're going to figure out what it is—or why—is to find more beads."

Evelyn and I spend the drive home chattering excitedly about what we should say on the flyer, and in which newspapers we should place ads. As we get closer to Evelyn and Dylan's house, though, there's one discussion we all know we can't delay any further.

Evelyn finally raises the topic: "So, I think we have to tell our parents."

I respond instantly. "No way. Do you know how *ticked* my mom will be? We drove all the way out to Danville, and lied about it. She'll ground me for life."

Dylan agrees. "I'm not getting in trouble for your little scheme. I was just helping out. You can't turn around now and fess up. I don't know about grounding for 'life,' but we'll get at least a week for sure, and I, for one, have plans this weekend."

I love my cousin. She's the best cousin a girl could ask for. But when she decides to adopt her perfect-angel routine, I'd gladly trade her in for somebody else. Right now is one of those times.

Evelyn sits back into her seat resolutely. "Well, I can't keep lying to my parents. I'm sorry, but if you want my help going forward, we'll have to tell them."

I groan in frustration. I do not want to do this alone. Well, okay, I wouldn't be alone. Chelsea and Emma have already said they'll help, but doing it without Ev?

"Fine," I finally say in a low growl. Then, when no one responds, I say it louder, "Fine. We can tell them. But next time you want to play Miss Goody Two Shoes, please let me know ahead of time."

Dylan doesn't give her a chance to respond, but pounds the steering wheel. "Last time I do you guys a favor! You'll never have any fun if you can't figure out how to keep a few details from your parents every once in a while!"

Evelyn lets out a loud laugh. "Ha! Yeah, look where it's gotten you! Every time you try to lie to Mom and Dad, they figure it out, and you wind up in trouble. In fact, it seems to me that you just got this little puppy back a few weeks ago," she says, running her hand over the dash of his car. "Thanks for your advice, Big Brother. I'll learn from your mistakes. We may have lied, but we're ending it here. Lies on top of lies will only make the problem—and the punishment—worse. If we come clean now, they'll appreciate our honesty, and—hopefully—won't be too hard on us."

Evelyn looks back at me with an angelic smile, batting her eyelashes, but her expression turns a little bit sick as she outlines her plan. "We tell them the truth. And you're right. We'll probably be grounded. So I guess it's a good thing that

Chelsea and Emma volunteered to put the flyers up, 'cause I don't see us getting out much for a while."

Call me a wimp, but I totally don't want to tell my parents by myself. I know that my mom had to run Gwen to softball practice, and Paul to baseball, so when we get back to Evelyn's house I call her and ask if she might be able to come pick me up after she drops them off, figuring that she'll come in to talk to Aunt Susan. That way, Evelyn, Dylan, and I can all stand before the judge and jury at the same time. My mom tends to be stricter than Aunt Susan, so I'm also hoping that Aunt Susan can talk her down from her first instinct on punishment, which will surely be grounding me for the rest of my life.

Evelyn and I hole up in her room to wait for my mom's arrival, and an eerie silence hangs over us. I open up *Lord of the Flies* again and pretend to read, but I can't concentrate. I literally feel sick to my stomach as I think about the discussion that's coming.

Finally, we hear my mom downstairs, calling for me to come down. We stop by Dylan's room, where Evelyn pokes her head around the door to let him know that it's time, and then the three of us slowly descend the stairs.

Mom and Aunt Susan are standing in the kitchen, talking. Evelyn clears her throat and begins our confession.

"Mom, Aunt Teresa, we need to talk to you."

The two women give each other a *look*, before looking back at the three of us. Aunt Susan glances at Dylan, clearly a little surprised that he would be involved in something Evelyn and I have been up to.

"Alright. Well, let's go into the living room, where we'll be more comfortable," Aunt Susan suggests, always cool-headed and an excellent hostess.

We walk into the living room. Mom and Aunt Susan take the two brocade armchairs, while Dylan, Evelyn, and I stand in front of the fireplace. I stare down at my hands, feeling like I should do the talking, since I got us into this mess. But, where do I begin?

"We didn't really go shopping today."

Mom and Aunt Susan both raise their eyebrows, and wait for me to say more.

A moment passes as I try to think about how to best tell the story. I think the "we were doing this for Aunt Liz" spin is probably best.

"We drove out to Danville, to the restaurant where we ate on Saturday after the . . . the memorial service."

I can see that Mom is getting a little ticked. "Katelyn, you *lied* to us? You *know* how serious that is!" she says.

"Yes, Mom, I know. I didn't want to—*we* didn't want to." I look at Evelyn and Dylan. "But we didn't really know enough of what was going on to feel like we could tell you about it." I gush on, "Something strange happened. When we were in that field on Saturday, and everyone was praying the Rosary, I walked over to a wooded area. Only, I didn't just *walk* over there. It was like I was *drawn* there. I didn't know why, but once I started, I just had to keep walking that way."

"What does this have to do with lying, Katelyn?" Mom's eyes flash with a combination of fear and anger.

"Let me tell you the rest," I blurt out, then collect myself to go on. "Once I got to the trees, there were a whole bunch of little purple flowers mixed in the grass. You know how Grandma loved flowers, right? Well, I looked down, and there was something shiny nestled in the flowers. I picked it up, and do you know what it was?" I pause, as if they're going to answer, "It was a bead from Grandma's rosary. It was *my* bead. K M R. My *bead*."

Aunt Susan gasps, and Mom's hand flutters to her mouth. I continue, "That's why I was in the trees for so long, and why it took me so long to come back to the car. I just couldn't believe it. So then we went to the restaurant, and the girl who was working in the gift shop—her name is Chelsea—saw me looking at it. She asked me what it was, and I told her. Then it got even weirder. Chelsea told me that she had found a bead just like mine, outside of the restaurant one day a while back. She gave it to her best friend, Emma, because it had her initials on it—E M L."

Mom sinks back into her chair and closes her eyes. Aunt Susan reaches over and grabs Mom's hand, and I see her eyes fill with tears. Grandma may not have been Aunt Susan's mother, but I know she misses her as much as the rest of us do.

I watch, letting the information sink in before I continue with Emma's story. Aunt Susan is the first to speak.

"Liz. It's Liz's bead, right?"

"Yep," Evelyn interjects. "We tried to call her last night, to see if maybe she could take us out to get the bead from Emma, and to hear Emma's story. But she never called us back."

Aunt Susan looks startled, then guilty. "Oh, Ev! She did call! She beeped in while I was on the other line, and I forgot all about it! I'm so sorry. I just forgot about it!"

"It's okay," Evelyn answers. "Dylan took us."

"None of this really explains why you *lied* to us," Mom says.

"I know," my shoulders sag, "but first, can I tell you the rest of the story?" I add, hopefully.

Mom crosses her arms and gives a short nod. The look on her face, though, makes it clear to me that she doesn't really want to hear anything more. I restart the story anyway.

"So when Chelsea told me about the bead, she also said that her friend, Emma, thought that the bead had saved her life. At first I wanted to get the bead back because it was from Grandma's rosary, and I thought Aunt Liz would want it. But when Chelsea said that bead could have saved a person's life, I just *had* to know how."

"Again, not an acceptable reason for lying. Why didn't you tell us?" Mom persists.

I wish I could shrink away and avoid this whole conversation. This is the last thing I want to talk about, especially in front of Aunt Susan, Evelyn, and Dylan. I stare at my hands to avoid looking her in the eye. "You've been so different since the plane crash. You're so sad, and mad all the time." I glance uneasily at the others in the room, not wanting to share secrets, but—let's face it—everyone has seen how she's changed. I'm not saying anything that everyone doesn't already know.

I steal a glance at Mom's shuttered face, then look back down at my hands. "I was afraid you'd tell me no, afraid you'd tell me that it was silly and that I was wasting my time. So, I didn't tell you, and I didn't tell Dad, because I knew he'd make me tell you. And I asked Evelyn not to tell anyone, either." I look at Mom again, and blink back tears. "I'm sorry," I whisper.

Mom stands. Clearly, I've said too much. "Kate, we'll discuss this further at home. It's time for us to go." She says a stiff goodbye to Aunt Susan, and then stalks from the room and out to the car.

I start to follow, keeping my face down so that they don't see the tears that are now streaming down my face. But I haven't fooled Aunt Susan. She walks over and gives me a hug.

"Kate, it'll be okay." She keeps her arms around me, and my tears quickly soak the fabric of the top she's wearing. "You'll see. Maybe this is just what your mom needs. Maybe this will help her." She puts her hands on my shoulders, gently pushing me away so that she can look straight into my eyes. "Kate, you need to pray. Pray for your mom. I will too." She gives me another quick squeeze and lets me go.

I nod to Aunt Susan and mumble goodbye to Evelyn and Dylan before I grab my backpack and head out the door. Mom's sitting in the driver's seat, hands gripping the steering wheel, with the engine running. She doesn't look at me as I climb into the car. She puts the car into gear, backs down the driveway, and we drive home in stony silence.

Chapter Six

"I still have to pick up your sister," Mom says as I open the car door. "Go to your room. I'll expect to find you there when I get home."

My stomach rumbles. I haven't had dinner yet and I'm starving. But I know better than to argue, so I go into the house and head straight up the stairs. Our dog, a yellow lab named Amber, seems to sense my mood and pads softly alongside me.

I grab a library book off of my bookshelf and sit down on my bed. Pillows behind my back, knees pulled up to rest the book on them, I try to focus on the story, reaching down occasionally to stroke Amber's head. But my mind wanders and I think about what Aunt Susan said. Pray for Mom. . . . Seriously? Why would I do that? It's not like she's praying for me. She's mad about something all the time, doesn't have anything nice to say, and is totally absorbed in herself and what losing Grandma did to *her.* Doesn't she realize that we're *all* hurting? She's not the only one who misses Grandma. I need to be able to talk about Grandma, about how wonderful she was, and laugh about her funny little quirks. I'd like to bake cookies and remember that it was Papa that did all the baking, or eat M&Ms and remember how Grandma would make a special trip out every day to buy herself a bag. But I can't! I don't get to do that because my mom—the person who is supposed to be doing these things with me—has shut me out, and shut everyone out, and—dang it!—I'm ticked off about it! So, no, I'm not going to pray for her! It's not like I sit around praying for people, anyway, and I'm certainly not going to start now! Not for *her*!!

I realize that I'm crying again. And now I'm angry with myself, angry for letting myself get all worked up over a mom who's stopped being a mom. I punch the bed, hard, but it doesn't make me feel any better. I try the pillows, and that doesn't help either. I throw the book across the room, and then I just feel silly, realizing that I'm throwing a temper tantrum like a three-year-old.

There's a knock at the door, and Gwen peeks her head in. I guess they're back. "Kate? Are you okay?"

I throw a pillow at her and yell, "Like you care!"

She ducks, slams the door, and shouts, "Well fine! If that's how you want to be!" before stomping down the hall.

An hour later, I'm making progress in my book when I hear the weight of Dad's footsteps approach my door. "Kate?" he says, his voice calm. "Can I come in?"

I don't answer, can't answer through the lump in my throat. "Kate?" he says, again. The door opens slowly and he steps into the room.

"Hey, sweetie." Dad grabs the box of tissues off my desk before he sits down on the edge of the bed. "Your mom told me about what happened."

I sniffle, still not ready to talk.

"You should have told us, sweetheart. You shouldn't have lied about where you were going or what you were doing." He puts his hand on my knee. "You *could* have told us."

I wrap my arms around myself. "I couldn't have told *her*. She would have told me I was stupid, that I was imagining things and dreaming it all up."

"Kate, your mom's having a rough time right now, but she never would have said that you're stupid. She loves you, even if she hasn't shown it very well lately."

"Yeah, well, I have a hard time believing that. Anyways, I told her, and now she won't even talk to me."

Dad looks out the window for a moment. "You know, Kate, we all understand that our parents are going to die someday. But we never expect that it's going to happen the way it did to Grandma. Your mom wasn't ready for that. None of us were ready for that. I know it's hard, Kate, and I wish you didn't have to go through all of this. But you have to be patient with Mom. She'll get through it. She will. And she'll be like the Mom she used to be. Just be patient, okay?" He squeezes my hand.

"In the meantime, I'll try to do better," Dad continues. "I should be home more. I'll try to work less, so I can be here for you and your brother and sister. Okay? Will that help?" I sniffle and nod my head. "Okay. Now, we do need to talk about the fact that you lied to us." He puts his fingers under my chin, forcing my gaze up to meet his. "Your mother and I feel very strongly about that. We've agreed that there does need to be a consequence, so you're grounded for a week." He says it gently, though, and I know he's not angry. A week is getting off pretty lightly, so I shrug my shoulders and nod my head, then look down again, uncomfortable holding his gaze. My stomach growls, and Dad lets out a little chuckle.

"You missed dinner, didn't you?" I smile and nod my head again. "Well, let's go do something about that." He stands and holds his hand out to me. I place my hand in his and he pulls me off the bed and into a giant bear hug. It feels good, and I finally relax a little bit. He's right. It'll be okay.

Dad fixes me a sandwich while I munch on grapes and tell him the story of everything that's happened with the bead. I tell him what I didn't get a chance to tell mom or Aunt Susan—about Emma's car crash. I also tell him that Evelyn and I are hoping to find the rest of the beads, and that Chelsea and Emma are going to help us.

"You know, Kate, I think that's a great idea. I'll tell you what," he puts down the knife that he's been using to smear mayonnaise. "You put together what you want the flyer to say, and I'll ask one of the graphic designers at the office to give it some zing." He puts the final touches on the sandwich and hands me the plate. "In fact, if you'd like, you can come into the office and tell them exactly what you want it to look like and they can show you how they do it. What d'you think?"

"Seriously?!" I nearly choke on my first bite of sandwich. "Dad, that would be awesome! When?" A designer from his web design company will be able to create a much better flyer than I could make on my own.

"Well, you *are* grounded, so we'll need to wait until that's up. We've also got some major client deadlines next week, but I believe those will all wrap up on Thursday. Why don't you plan on coming in on Friday after school. I'll see if your mom can give you a ride."

Okay, well that's a damper, but I'm still pretty excited. I start to chatter about what I think the flyer should say, and Dad tells me to put it on the computer and e-mail it to him when I'm done. I finish up my sandwich, then call Evelyn so that I can consult her about the flyer.

"Kate! Are you okay? Your mom was *ticked!*"

"Yeah. She sent me to my room and hasn't talked to me since. Did you get in trouble?"

"Yeah, Dylan and I are both grounded for a week. How 'bout you?"

"Same here. But, listen to this! My dad's going to have one of his graphic designers help us with the flyer!"

"Seriously?" Evelyn squeals, "Oh my gosh! How cool is that!"

"Yep! He's going to check schedules, but he thinks I can come in next Friday after school. So now we just need to figure out what we want it to say. Can you help me?"

I head downstairs so that I can use the computer as we start brainstorming ideas for the flyer. Finally, we have it down:

Lost Beads

Very special to family who lost a loved one
in the Danville plane crash.
Each bead is silver, with engraved initials
and a cross.
Also seeking lost crucifix and rosary medallion.

I add my e-mail address and phone number to the bottom, and send it to my dad's work e-mail address with a satisfied flourish.

When we're finished, Evelyn shares more news.

"My mom called Aunt Liz. She was at the airport in Chicago, headed back to Denver. Mom told her that we found the bead. She was really excited, but doesn't want us to mail it, just in case something happens and it gets lost. She wants you to hold onto it until she comes next month for Easter."

"Okay," I say, nodding my head.

Evelyn continues, "My mom called Uncle Joseph, too. She wanted to ask him what he thought about finding the beads—because he's a priest, you know?"

"Yeah, I guess that makes sense. What did he say?"

"Well, you probably ought to talk with him yourself, but Mom said something about him being concerned that we might think the beads were *magical* or something. He said the beads don't possess any power of their own. He said that Grandma was always close to the Blessed Mother, and that maybe they're both praying for whoever has the bead. He says that's where the power comes from—prayer—because God is always listening. I guess that makes sense, doesn't it?"

I'm not sure that it *does* make sense, but pretend that I get it, anyways. We hang up, and I head to my room. I sit down at my desk, remove the necklace from around my neck, and sit for several moments rolling the two beads around in my palm.

"Grandma?" I say quietly. "I don't know if you can hear me, but I sure do miss you. I wish you were here." I pause. "Are you praying with Mary? Did you two save Emma in that car accident?" I pause again, like I'm waiting for her to answer. "Grandma, did you lead me to the bead? W*hy*?" So many questions. "Will you help us find the rest of them?" I look up at the ceiling, as if I might see her there. "Please, help us find them." Finally, I whisper, "And, Grandma? Please help Mom. She needs it."

I sit there thinking for a bit, and it strikes me that it isn't right for me to keep both of these beads. Evelyn's in on this too, and she should have one of them, at least until we have to give it to Aunt Liz. Besides, two of the three initials match Evelyn's. I rifle through my jewelry box, find another chain, and slide Aunt Liz's bead onto it. I stick the chain in a pocket of my backpack, intent on giving it to Evelyn at school tomorrow.

The day dawns wet and cooler than yesterday. I wake up late, so I skip my shower and settle for brushing my teeth, splashing water on my face, and pulling my hair back into a ponytail. I throw my uniform shirt and khakis on, for once thankful that I don't have to worry about what to wear.

I yank a sweatshirt off the top shelf of my closet, pulling it on as I run down the stairs. I hold my backpack over my head as I race through the rain to the car, where Mom, Paul, and Gwen are already waiting. Mom doesn't say a word, but silently throws the car into reverse and backs down the driveway, making it clear that she's still angry with me.

We drop off Paul and Gwen at their school first, and Mom remains quiet as we drive across the street to my school, Bishop Chatard. As the rain picks up, its deafening noise fills the car to make the silence less awkward. I wonder idly if Evelyn was able to get a ride from Dylan, or if she's stuck walking in this mess.

I receive my answer when I get to my locker and spy Evelyn, soaked to the bone despite the umbrella that she's hanging up. Aunt Susan's pretty cool, but she sticks to the "I walked to school and so can you" rule. It's only a few blocks, but those few blocks can be pretty brutal in a driving rain.

Evelyn looks up from the umbrella, which is now dripping in her locker, and sees me watching her. She pushes her wet hair out of her face and gives a huff. Clearly, this is not her best day ever. I wordlessly remove my sweatshirt and hand it to her. At least she'll have one dry item of clothing on. Then, I remember the necklace that's tucked in my backpack.

Evelyn gives me a grateful smile and quickly dons the sweatshirt, then rubs her arms to warm them through the material. I pull the necklace from the backpack pocket and hold it out in the palm of my hand.

"For you," I say. "At least until we give it to Aunt Liz. And find yours." I smile, pleased with myself.

"Really?" Her smile widens. "Huh. Funny, I hadn't even thought about the fact that we might find *my* bead. I guess we really could, couldn't we?"

"We're sure gonna try," I say. The bell rings, and we realize that we're late for class. "Uh oh! Gotta go!" I say. We both grab our books and run.

The days pass slowly as I wait for the following Friday to come, when I'll finally get to go to Dad's office to work on the flyer.

I call Chelsea on Tuesday to give her the news about the flyer and ask her about placing an ad in the newspaper. She says that there's a local weekly paper that might work. I call them on Wednesday, but their deadline has passed and the earliest they can run the ad is next Friday. Evelyn and Aunt Susan come up with the idea of putting something on Craig's List. They get that up and running, but with no immediate results.

Friday finally rolls around and Mom takes me straight to Dad's office after school. She's barely talked to me since last Monday—or anyone else, for that matter. I can't believe she doesn't want to know the rest of the story about Emma's bead, but maybe Dad told her. I find myself wishing, once again, that I could have my old mom back.

Mom used to be really great, involved in what we did without being *too* involved; ready to listen to my problems and offer advice, without cramming her ideas down my throat. We used to have family game night, family movie night, family hikes, and family dinners, but that's all pretty much stopped since Grandma died a year ago.

Mom drops me off at the door, and I walk up to the receptionist, feeling a bit awkward. She calls my dad to let him know that I've arrived, and he comes out of his office to greet me.

"How was your day, sweetheart?" He asks as he releases me from a hug.

"Good. I think my French test went well."

"I'm sure it did. You always do well in school. Your mom and I are proud of you."

I scuffle my feet and stare at my shoes.

"Come on, let me introduce you to Natalie." He puts an arm around my shoulders and ushers me back to the graphic design area, filled with messy desks and artsy-looking people. As we approach, a woman with cat's eye glasses and curly red hair which is doing its best to escape a messy bun looks up and gives me a friendly smile. She stands and shakes my hand.

"Hi! You must be Katelyn. I'm Natalie."

"Hi," I say, looking at our joined hands. Then, remembering my manners, I look her in the eye and say, "It's nice to meet you."

"The pleasure's mine," Natalie answers with a smile. "This sounds like a pretty cool project."

Dad leaves us to it. Natalie pulls over another chair and gestures for me to sit as she pulls up the flyer I drafted while I was on the phone with Evelyn. I look around her cubicle, taking notice of a crucifix hanging to the left of her big, fancy-looking computer screen. Hanging nearby is a copy of the Saint Francis prayer I learned in kindergarten, the one we sing so often at Mass. *Make me a channel of your peace. . . .*

Natalie's easy manner and quick smile had already put me at ease, but, seeing the crucifix and prayer, I take a deep breath realizing that I'm with someone who *gets it*. I think about how cool it is that Dad would team me up with her, even though he's not Catholic, and how funny it is that I'm so glad to see these symbols, when they've never really meant much to me before.

"Okay," Natalie says, opening a file on her computer. "First, let me tell you that I'm very sorry about your grandmother. I lost my grandma last year too, and I know how hard that is." I blink back tears, amazed, as always, at how much the kind words of others affect me.

"But," she continues, "it sounds like your Grandma was a special person who really believed in the power of prayer. I'm honored to be able to help you find what you're looking for. So, let's take a look at this flyer."

We spend the next hour setting a background, changing font styles and sizes, and adding decorative elements. We take photos of my bead, upload them to her computer, and pick two to add to the flyer. By the end, we've got an eye-catching flyer that people will surely pause to look at.

Finally, Natalie shocks me by saying, "Okay. I think we've got it. Now, the last thing, and the most important thing, is for us to pray." She bows her head, folds her hands, and makes the Sign of the Cross.

"Heavenly Father, thank you for giving Katelyn the grace of discovering the beads from her grandmother's rosary. We believe that these beads are signs of your presence and goodness. If it is your will, Lord, we ask that you bless Katelyn's mission. We ask that you draw people to read and consider this flyer, especially the people who have found any of the missing beads. Blessed Mother, we know that praying the Rosary is a great weapon in the fight to win souls for your Son, Jesus Christ. This rosary is only a material thing, but it reminds us of Katelyn's grandmother and her loving prayers for her family. Please help Katelyn and her family not only to find these beads, but also to find healing and peace in their loss. We ask this in the name of the Father, and of the Son, and of the Holy Spirit. Amen. Saint Dominic, to whom the Rosary was given, pray for us. Saint Anthony, Finder of Lost Articles, pray for us."

I make the Sign of the Cross with Natalie, and sit for a moment, speechless but hopeful. Much more hopeful than I had been *before* that prayer, when—if I were honest with myself—I felt like we were looking for a needle in a haystack. Now, it seems like we've got more than just me and Evelyn on our side.

As we drive home, Dad offers to take the two of us out to Danville early next week to post the flyers. I'm about to bubble over with excitement, until Dad receives a text from mom. "Going shopping. Paul sleeping over at Ryan's, Gwen at Sophie's. Pizza in freezer."

Dad pats my knee and asks, "How about getting a movie and some popcorn? You choose the movie." He looks at me hopefully and I realize that he's probably missing the old Mom just as much as I am. My friends and I had talked about going to a movie, but it's one I've already seen, so it won't be a huge loss to stay at home with Dad. We stop by a rental box and I pick out a movie I missed in the theaters. Dad gets some microwave popcorn, just in case we're out at home, and a two-liter bottle of soda—a special treat, since Mom doesn't keep any in the house.

Mom comes home while we're curled up on either end of the couch, pizza devoured and popcorn bowl between us. The laughter we share in response to a funny scene in the movie breaks off abruptly as we hear the back door open. I glance at Dad, but his eyes are trained on the TV. As he attempts to rearrange his face into a pleasant smile, it's clear that he's not sure what to make of Mom's terse text.

Mom doesn't even say hello, just pauses briefly on her way through the living room. "I bought a new book. I'll be upstairs reading," she says in a flat voice. She disappears up the stairs.

I look at Dad again. His lips form a grim line across his face, and his chin is set. We continue to watch the movie for a few more minutes, but there's no more laughter now. We're both lost in our own thoughts.

I think of the woman my mother used to be, a woman who would never have taken off on a Friday night, but who would have planned this movie night herself, complete with a make-your-own pizza party and a catch-the-popcorn-in-your-mouth contest. As tears begin to fill my eyes, I idly toss a piece of popcorn to the dog, but barely muster a smile when she deftly jumps to catch it.

I slide off the couch to the floor and open my arms to Amber. She comes willingly, and the seventy-pound dog winds up in my lap—her favorite spot. I bury my face in the soft blond fur of her neck, wishing that all of this would just go away. If Grandma's rosary beads are going to drive Mom further away from us, I wish I hadn't found them. I begin to wonder if maybe I should just stop the search.

Dad gets up quietly, squeezes my shoulder, and heads up the stairs. I hear their bedroom door open and close, and within a few minutes I hear raised voices. I grab the remote, turn the volume way up on the movie, and stare at the television screen. I try to focus, to make myself laugh at the funny parts, but the best I can manage is a smile that feels more like a grimace. Finally, things are quiet upstairs, so I turn the TV off and head to bed, hoping that sleep will bring relief from my emotions, and that tomorrow dawn will bring a better day.

✎

I find myself standing in a recently planted field. Tiny, bright-green seedlings stretch out before me in every direction. I look to my left and see two people standing in the distance. I begin to walk toward them, careful to avoid crushing the tiny plants under my feet. Suddenly, the nice, neat rows of seedlings are gone, and the ground is covered in the plants, but they're growing rapidly, wrapping around my feet as I walk, trying to hold me in place. I look toward the two women and realize that one of them is Grandma, beckoning me. Each step is a struggle, as I disentangle my feet from the grasping plants, which are now trying to climb like vines up my legs.

Suddenly, I'm standing at the edge of a pond, and Grandma and the other woman are just on the other side. Still, Grandma motions me on. I dive into the water and kick up into the air. As my head clears the surface, I realize that the pond is not water anymore, but a sea of beads. I find that I am buoyant on them, and they are propelling me toward the other side. Within moments, I'm washed up onto the shore in a tidal wave of beads—green, blue, pink, silver—every color imaginable. I look back to see that the pond is no longer small, but now a vast sea of beads, glistening and reflecting the light of the sun, and stretching out to the horizon as far as the eye can see. I turn to Grandma, wanting to embrace her, but somehow my feet won't move. I see that she's holding her rosary in her hand, smiling gently at me. Her other hand holds that of the woman standing beside her. The woman is beautiful, dressed in a blue robe, with a face that breathes love and eyes that whisper peace. The hand that doesn't clasp my grandmother's holds a rosary as well. The two women look upward and begin to pray the Our Father; their faces fill with rapture. I realize that I, too, am holding a rosary, and it's just like Grandma's. I open my mouth to join in their prayer, wanting to share in their bliss, but the words won't come. I look at Grandma, *wanting to ask her to help me. She smiles, looks deep into my eyes, and says, "It will come, Kate. It will come."*

I wake with a start and find that I'm clasping the single rosary bead in my hand. The clock reads two thirty, and I lay awake, trying to remember every detail of the dream. Forty-five minutes later, as I finally drift back to sleep, I feel a peace and calm that I haven't felt in a long time. I know what I must do. I must keep looking for the remaining beads.

Chapter Seven

Tuesday, Dad picks me and Evelyn up from school, and we head to Danville to post flyers. Unfortunately, Gwen and Paul both wanted to come as well, so the car is full and noisy as Gwen chatters away about every minute detail of her day. We're on a tight schedule—Evelyn and Gwen have softball practice, and Paul has baseball—and I'm grateful when Dad suggests that we should work on our homework in the car. Dad plugs his phone into the car's audio adapter and instructs me to play his classical music mix. Gwen finally quiets down as the car fills with the soothing strains of some centuries-old orchestral piece.

The drive flies by, each of us focused on the evening's homework, and I've still got tons more to do when we pull up in front of the Mayberry Café. We meet Chelsea and Emma inside, and decide to break into groups to distribute flyers. Emma and Chelsea are going to drive over to the grocery store, and also hit a few other shops and restaurants while they're over that way. Evelyn, Gwen, and I are going to try the shops on the north side of the street, and Dad and Paul are going to take care of the south side.

Danville's "downtown" area isn't much to write home about, so in no time at all, we've covered the few stores, the bakery, and the tailor. We also tape a few to the light posts that line the road. Once that's done, we meet back up and agree to drive around town, searching for other possible public spaces where we might be able to post the flyers. We find the library and historic center, but still have lots of flyers left. Finally, we decide to drive near the field where the plane went down and leave flyers on the mailboxes of the homes in the area.

One way or another, this has to turn up a few beads. Now, we wait.

For the first two days, I had a hard time leaving the phone because I kept hoping that someone would call. When I came home from school each day, the first thing I did was run and check for voicemail messages, then jump on the computer to check e-mail.

Now it's Friday, and I still haven't heard a word. Evelyn and I are hanging out at my house, playing pool in the basement, with the cordless phone a few feet away on an end table. I am just lining up a shot that I'm quite confident is going to be the most amazing shot *ever* when the phone rings. I nearly jump out of my skin and whiff the side of the white ball, which sends it careening into Evelyn's 11 ball, which sails across the table, straight into the pocket. Great.

Funny, I've been waiting for the phone to ring all week, and now, when it finally does, I find myself staring at it as if it might be an alien, or perhaps a poisonous snake. Evelyn finally walks over to the table, snatches up the phone, and intones, "Roberts' residence!" Her eyes widen. "Katelyn? Why, yes! She's right here! Just a moment!" She presses her palm into the mouthpiece and gives a little squeal. "It's for you! Do you think it could be—"

"I don't know!" I nervously cut her off. I grab the phone from her hand. "Hello?" I say in a small voice that doesn't sound like my own.

"Hi, Katelyn! It's Natalie, from your dad's office!" My shoulders slouch in disappointment. Natalie continues, "I just wanted to call and see if you've heard anything yet from the flyers you posted?"

"No," I say, disappointment lacing my voice. "We put them up on Tuesday, and we still haven't gotten a single call."

"Humph. Well, let's see. What else can we do?" I can envision Natalie tapping her fingers on her chin the way she did several times while we were designing the flyer. Then, after an awkward moment of silence, she says, "Have you prayed?"

"What?" I'm a bit taken aback. This is the best she can do? "Um, no, not since you did on Friday."

"I'll tell you what. You pray about it, and I'll pray about it, and let's see if that gets us anywhere. Okay?"

"Okay. Sure." Yeah, right. "Thanks."

"No problem. I'll talk to you soon, okay? Call me if you hear anything."

I assure her that I will and roll my eyes as I press the end button. I turn to Evelyn.

"That was Natalie. She's the one from my dad's office that designed the flyer. Her brilliant suggestion is that we should pray." I pick up my pool cue and wait for Evelyn to resume the game, but she just leans on her cue and raises her eyebrows at me.

"What?" I question, slightly irritated.

"I can't believe I didn't think of it before. Duh!"

"Ev, you can't be serious. Okay, fine. Dear God, please help us find a bead. Amen." I quickly cross myself and turn back to the pool table.

"Come on, Kate! You can't be *that* jaded. I think a little respect might be nice for starters. 'Dear God,'" she mimics in a funny voice, making it clear what she thinks of my little prayer. "We *are* looking for *rosary* beads. So perhaps a Hail Mary might be in order?"

"Sure." This time I start with the Sign of the Cross, exaggerating the gestures and saying the words slowly. Then I steeple my hands, look heavenward, and pray the Hail Mary. And this time something happens. My dream comes rushing back to me, and I can vividly see Grandma and the other woman praying the Rosary. I take a step backwards, feel my legs hit a chair, and sag against its thick, upholstered arm. My hand reaches up to feel the bead hanging from around my neck.

"What! What is it?" Evelyn asks anxiously.

"I . . . I had this dream. Grandma and a . . . a woman were praying the Rosary," and I proceed to tell her about it—the field, the vines trying to hold me down, the pond that turned to beads, and Grandma . . . and the woman . . . and the prayer. "And then Grandma said, 'It will come, Kate. It will come.'" I breathe raggedly, finishing the story.

I don't know why I hadn't told Evelyn before. I guess it just felt too personal and weird, and like a silly dream that, in the bright light of day, probably didn't really mean anything.

"Kate! You are *so* dense sometimes! Do you realize who '*the woman*' was?"

I look at Evelyn scathingly. "Yes, Evelyn. I do. It was Mary." But to be honest, I hadn't really admitted that to myself until just now.

Evelyn gives a shrill shriek and grabs my arms, hauling me off the arm of the chair. "Kate, you had a *vision*! You had a vision of *the Blessed Mother*!" She says these last words slowly, and shakes me as she does.

"Ev, come on. Don't blow this out of proportion. It was a *dream*. A *dream* and a *vision* are two different things. I was *asleep*."

"Okay, okay, okay. Whatever. You saw Mary. She appeared to you in a dream. I mean, seriously! It all has to mean something. The plants entangling around your feet? Maybe that's like—everything that's trying to hold you back from doing this! And the beads, and them praying the Rosary? I don't know! Maybe the beads in the ocean are a symbol of every Rosary that's ever been prayed, or something. And Grandma and the Blessed Mother—they were *showing* you what to do! They were *telling you* to pray the Rosary!"

Leave it to Evelyn, who consistently gets an A+ in English class, to overinterpret my dream.

"Ev, it was just a dream. It was probably my subconscious thinking through everything that's been going on. I mean, I have been thinking about rosaries and Grandma an awful lot lately, and Mary comes right along with the Rosary, doesn't she? It didn't *mean* anything, but it did make me want to keep looking when I was just about ready to give up."

Now Evelyn grabs my hand and pulls me toward the stairs. "Where's your rosary?" She asks.

"Geesh. I don't know. I put it somewhere after First Communion. That was a long time ago."

"You haven't prayed a Rosary since First Communion, in *second grade*? You've got to be kidding me."

Evelyn, as you may have guessed, does not share my reservations about religion. I mean, she's no saint, but she's pretty much into the Catholic stuff. So she drags me upstairs and heads into the kitchen, where we dropped our bags when we got home. She rummages through her backpack and, after a few moments, pulls out her rosary with a flourish. Then she heads up to my room and starts opening drawers, searching, but failing to find my long-neglected rosary.

Then memory hits. I go to the closet and pull my keepsake box down off the top shelf. Opening the lid, I see a small green silk pouch nestled in the midst of the cards, buttons, and dried flowers. I hold it up for Evelyn to see, feeling a bit smug.

I unsnap the bag and pull out the rosary, looking at the crucifix and beads a bit wonderingly. Grandma gave this to me for my first Communion. Have I ever actually prayed on these beads? I don't think so.

Well, I guess there's a first for everything.

Still skeptical, I sit down on the floor, legs crossed, with my back resting against the bed. Evelyn looks around the room as if something's missing. Then she leaves the room, coming back with the candle from the bathroom and a book of matches. I can't help but roll my eyes. She pretends not to see me, though I'm quite certain she did. Evelyn sets the candle on the bedside table, and kneels at the side of the bed, with her rosary beads in hand. She looks over at me, sitting there on the floor, and clears her throat. Reluctantly, I rise up onto my knees and turn around, kneeling beside her.

Evelyn leads and I follow along, fumbling through several of the prayers. Fifteen minutes later, we're done, but both of us continue to kneel in silence. I feel calm and peaceful, no longer worrying about when someone's going to call, or whether anyone's going to call at all. I savor that feeling for several minutes, before sitting back down on the floor. Evelyn follows me and we sit companionably, leaning against the bed.

I finally break the silence. "Wow. That was pretty impressive."

"What?" Evelyn asks in surprise.

"You. You know the whole Rosary. Like, even the mysteries and stuff."

Evelyn seems a little uncomfortable. "Yeah, well," she shrugs, "my family prays the Rosary together every Sunday. So I've heard it a bazillion times."

"Seriously?" I glance at her, as if she would lie about such a thing. "Huh. That's cool, I guess." I wonder how different my family might be right now if we prayed a Rosary every Sunday.

Evelyn thinks for a moment too, then, "Yeah, I used to hate it, but now, since I've gotten older, I kind of like it. Especially after Grandma died . . . It helped me deal with losing her, you know?" She shrugs her shoulders and continues, "We all share our prayer intentions before, and it just feels good to have everyone praying together like that."

We continue to sit silently until we're jarred by the "brnnng!" of the phone. Both of us jump to our feet.

This time, I don't hesitate. The caller ID reads, *Danville, IN*. My heart feels like it's going to jump right out of my chest as I push the button on the cordless handset and press the phone to my ear.

"Hello?" I try to look down at the phone as it rests against my chin, as if I'll be able to see the caller.

"Hello. Is Katelyn there?" A man asks in a jovial voice that carries the slight twang of rural Indiana.

I jump up and down and grab hold of Evelyn's hand. "Yes, this is Kate."

"Oh, great. Well, my name is Roger Billings. I own the field where that plane crash occurred. I was in the grocery store earlier today and saw your flyer. Found one on my mailbox too, actually, but I seem to have misplaced that one. Anyways, I believe I found a few of the beads you're looking for. Silver, with three letters engraved on them?"

"Yes, that's right."

"Yep, I found them, alright, in odd places around the field. I don't know how the investigators missed them, but they did. I figured they'd have no good use for them, so I gave them to my granddaughter. She's just a little thing—four years old—and she loves anything shiny or sparkly, so I thought she'd really get a kick out of 'em. Plus, her initials matched one of the beads. H L L, for Hannah Lynn Layton. I thought that was pretty special."

"Huh!" I say in a surprised laugh. Another bead found, another person with matching initials. Only, I can't think of anyone in our family who has the initials, H L L. I frown in concentration, and Evelyn is trying to figure out what's going on. I grab a piece of paper and jot down, H L L?, then look expectantly at my cousin. Evelyn purses her lips, thinks for a moment, then gives a little jump, and folds her arms together as if she were holding a baby.

That's it! It's one of the babies Grandma lost.

Mr. Roger Billings has continued to talk, and I've totally missed everything he's said. I tune back in, trying to pick up on what I've missed, but no such luck.

"Yep, so that's it. That's all I know." He wraps up his end of the conversation.

"Um, so, Mr. Billings, would it be possible for us to get the beads back from Hannah?"

"Well, hon, like I said, they live down in Florida, so that's easier said than done. And, well, I've gotta tell you, my daughter . . . well, she seems to feel the beads have some sort of, well . . ." he chuckles, sounding a bit embarrassed. But I know what's coming. "Well, this is gonna sound crazy, but she thinks they've got some sort of power."

I think my eyes are going to pop out of my head. "Mr. Billings, can we come and talk with you? I really want to hear more about this. I'll have to see if my dad can take me and my cousin out there, but if he can, would you be able to meet tomorrow?"

As we end the conversation and I hang up the phone, I realize that my rosary beads are still entwined around my hand. I stare at them in wonder. Was it just a coincidence, or did our prayer actually *work*? Evelyn and I lock gazes. From the look on her face, I know that she believes the phone call was the direct result of our prayer.

Could she be right?

Chapter Eight

The next morning, Dad insists that I drive. I've had my learner's permit for nearly a year, and I'm supposed to take the exam in August to get my license. The learner's permit means that I can drive, as long as one of my parents is in the passenger seat. I used to drive all the time, but then I had a little mishap with an oncoming car, and I haven't driven since. Today, however, Dad says that I've "got to get back up on the horse," whatever that means, and that the only way we're going out to Danville is if I drive.

I slide behind the wheel, filled with unease. My heart is beating so hard and fast, I'm sure Dad can hear it, and my palms are sweaty on the steering wheel. I know my stops and starts are jerky as we head to Evelyn's house, but Dad doesn't say anything. When she sees that I'm driving, Evelyn quirks an eyebrow in surprise, but she doesn't say anything either as she climbs into the backseat.

I finally begin to get over my nervousness as we drive down 38th Street. Traffic isn't bad this early on a Saturday, and the lights are timed, so I can cruise at a pretty constant speed. Spring has finally arrived, and we ride with the windows down, letting the wind whip through our hair. The fresh air feels great, and I breathe deeply, looking forward to summer and all it has to offer. One of Dad's old-time favorites, Led Zeppelin, is streaming across the radio. He leans his head back in the seat, humming softly, with his eyes closed. He seems to relax more the further we drive, and I wonder whether he's getting more comfortable with my driving, or if he's just relieved to be getting away from Mom.

It's been a tense week at our house, and I, for one, am really happy to have an excuse to get away. She's not even trying to pretend that everything's okay anymore, and at times I feel like she's about to shatter into a million pieces. I am not okay with having a mother who ought to be covered in bubble wrap and labeled with a giant, "FRAGILE: Handle with Care" sticker.

I try not to think about her as we drive through Danville and then follow country roads toward Roger Billings' house. Dad lets the map on his phone guide the way, but repeats every direction the computerized voice gives. Finally, I turn carefully onto a gravel drive. The rocks crunch under the tires and hit the bottom of the car. I know Dad must be freaking out over the mess that is being made of his beloved sedan. When I look over at him, his jaw is set, but then he notices me watching him, and gives me a smile.

"Should've taken your mom's car," he jokes. I laugh and agree with him.

We pull up to a tidy, white farm house, which must be over a century old. Several large trees in the front yard are budding to life with the season, and spring flowers are bursting from the ground. As we climb from the car, the front door opens and an old, friendly looking man in jeans, plaid shirt, and suspenders steps through.

"Well, hello there!" the man beams, coming out to meet us on the lawn.

"Hello, Mr. Billings. My name is Mike Roberts. I'm Katelyn's dad." The two men shake hands vigorously before turning to me and Evelyn. "This is Kate," he puts his hand on my shoulder, "and her cousin, Evelyn." He motions to Evelyn, standing beside me.

"How do you do, ladies? It's a pleasure to meet you." Mr. Billings offers his hand to me. I take it and feel the rough grip of a man who has known many years of hard work outdoors.

After shaking Evelyn's hand, Mr. Billings climbs the stairs heavily and invites us to sit on the wide front porch. He excuses himself and disappears inside, returning a moment later with a pitcher of lemonade and glasses.

"We don't get many visitors out here. My wife, Judy, used to just love it when someone stopped by. She insisted that we have these chairs out here, and she made lemonade and cookies anytime we were expecting company. I'm not much for baking cookies, though maybe you wouldn't guess it from the looks of me," he chuckles and pats his ample belly, "but I figure I can mix powder and water as well as anyone else to make up some lemonade."

"It's very kind of you, Mr. Billings," Dad answers.

"Please, call me Roger. We're not fancy people out here." He pulls a chair around, so that we're all facing each other conversationally.

"Roger, then. Well, first, thank you for having us out today. I understand from Kate that you found three of the missing beads, and that your granddaughter has them now?"

"Yes, that's right. Her name's Hannah. She's four years old, and I'll admit I spoil the girl. Give her everything she wants, when I get to see her. She's been sick her whole life, and, with everything she's been through, I just never want to say no to her." Mr. Billings sits back in his chair thoughtfully. "But things do seem to be lookin' up," he smiles at me, "ever since I gave those beads to her."

"Really?" I sit forward in my seat, and speak for the first time. "What happened?"

"Well, you see, Hannah's been too sick to travel for a long, long time, so the only time I get to see her is when I go there to visit, which, unfortunately, is only a few times a year. I found those beads last summer, and the next time I went out was in November, for Thanksgiving. I brought the beads with me, and I gave them to Hannah. Her mom got a ribbon and made a little necklace, with those three beads. Hannah had been undergoin' another treatment, and she was terribly sick. She couldn't keep anything she ate down, and had gotten real, real thin. It was awful to see her like that." Mr. Billings stares out toward the empty field at the side of the house, pain in his eyes as he remembers his granddaughter's pain. "She started wearin' those beads, though, and—not long afterward—she perked up. I had arrived on Monday, and by Thanksgiving on Thursday, she was able to sit at the table with the rest of us and eat dinner! You talk about somethin' to be *grateful* for! Well, we had it." His eyes fill with tears. He blinks rapidly several times and takes a deep drink from his glass.

Mr. Billings stares into his lemonade. "The doctors couldn't explain the sudden turnaround—said they'd never seen anything like it. My daughter, Melanie, thinks it had something to do with the beads."

I nod my head, speechless. Dad says, "Roger, I've got to tell you, I'm not a big believer in these things, but the girls seem to think that your daughter could be right."

Dad briefly tells him Emma's story, and Evelyn and I add a few details. "Kate found the bead with her initials on it. We haven't seen any miracles yet, though," Dad shrugs, clearly skeptical. Then, "Roger, we would never ask Hannah to give those beads back." I nearly choke on my lemonade in protest, but Dad continues, "Whether or not they are behind her doing better, they're special to her. I do wonder, though, if you know—or could find out—what initials are on the other two beads?"

Evelyn sits forward in her chair, a jumble of emotions crossing her face. I realize that she desperately wants to find her own bead, but if it's one of the beads Hannah has, Dad's just destroyed her hope of actually being able to have it for herself.

Mr. Billings thinks for a moment. "Well, Mike, I really don't remember. But I can call Melanie, and have her check. Give me a minute." He stands and walks into the house.

We sit in an awkward silence as we wait. Suddenly we hear a whoop from the house, and look at each other with our eyebrows raised. Mr. Billings returns a few minutes later, his face lit up with a huge smile and a new energy in his step.

"It's gone! The cancer's gone!" He shares excitedly. "They did a scan yesterday, and the doctor just called with the results. He didn't want to wait till Monday. It's gone!" He grabs me from my chair in a giant bear hug and swoops me around in a circle.

Startled at first, by the time he sets me down I share his excitement. I feel like my face might crack, my smile is so big. Those stupid tears that have come too often lately are back again, only this time they're happy tears, and I let them fall down my cheeks unchecked. Evelyn's next for a big bear hug, and then Dad stands and offers his hand.

"Congratulations, Roger," he says, as Mr. Billings grabs his hand and pulls Dad in for a huge hug of his own. Now, we're all laughing, the two men thumping each other on the back, as we all enjoy the moment of celebration. We've just met Mr. Billings, and have never met little Hannah, but somehow, this seems like a special victory for all of us.

Finally, once we calm down, Mr. Billings fishes a piece of paper from his pocket. "I did get those other initials for you." Unfolding the paper, he holds it out to me.

Evelyn beats me to it and snatches it from his hand. I see a strange mixture of relief and disappointment as she reads the letters, sags against her chair, and hands the note to me.

J E L

T M L

It takes me a minute to realize that the first one is probably another one of the babies Grandma miscarried.

The second set of initials hits me like a ton of bricks. I know instantly who they belong to. T M L, Teresa Michelle Langford, or at least that's who she was before she married my dad.

My lips twist in a bitter grimace, and I blink back still more tears. If these beads are somehow connected to miracles, could this one bring my mother back to me?

We stay a little bit longer, as Dad and Evelyn talk with Mr. Billings, but I don't have much to add to the conversation. As we prepare to leave, Dad offers me the keys, but doesn't argue when I shake my head and head for the passenger seat. We stop in at the Mayberry Café to see Chelsea, but she's not there, so we pile right back into the car and hit the road toward home.

I stare out the window as we drive, but I don't notice the beauty of the changing season. I play with the bead around my neck, lost in my thoughts as the miles drag past, littered with stoplights and traffic. Dad stops along the road and gets us each a milkshake, but my stomach is still growling when we pull up at Evelyn's house to drop her off.

"Do you want to grab lunch somewhere?" Dad asks as we pull away from Evelyn's house.

Not eager to return home to Mom and whatever mood may hold her, I murmur a soft "yes." Dad sighs heavily and drives to Binkley's.

It's late for lunch, and the restaurant is mostly deserted. We get a table by the fireplace, one of my favorite spots in this restaurant that has been converted from an old pharmacy into a neighborhood gathering place. I order a soda and a cheeseburger, of course, while Dad opts for a pork tenderloin sandwich.

After the waitress delivers our drinks, Dad leans on the table and looks at me closely. I look down at the napkin on the table in front of me, pleating it with my fingers.

"You've been awfully quiet," he probes.

I shake my head, not looking at him, and continue to play with the napkin.

"Come on, Kate. What's wrong?" he asks.

"Mom's bead." I finally manage in a strangled voice. Then, I look him in the eye, angry. "She has *Mom's* bead."

He sits back in his seat as realization dawns. "Kate, we can't take those beads from that little girl."

"But, Dad! It's not even the one with her initials on it!" I cry out, angrily, "It's not *her* bead! None of them are, really. But she can keep the one with her initials on it. That person's dead—barely even lived! But we *need* Mom's!" I pound my fist on the table, looking him full in the face now. "Mom's gone! She's *gone*, Dad! How else are we going to get her back?"

"Kate, what are you talking about? Your Mom isn't gone. She's at home, probably doing laundry as we speak."

"You know what I mean, Dad. Ever since Grandma died, she's not the same person. She just mopes around, doing *laundry*, or the *cleaning*, or reading some stupid book, as if that's more important to her than any of us. She's mean, and she doesn't pay any attention to any of us, especially not me. She doesn't love any of us anymore, and she *hates me*!"

"Kate, your mother does *not* hate you. She loves you. She's just . . . she's having a hard time right now." He takes my hand across the table, and gives it a gentle squeeze before releasing it. "Sweetie, I don't know why losing your Grandma has hit your mom so hard, and I don't know why this whole rosary bead thing is upsetting her so much. But your mom's always been a strong person. She'll bounce back from this. She will."

I shake my head, tears dripping from my eyes as I hang my head, trying to hide them from anyone who might be looking. Dad tries again.

"Honey, there's a natural grieving process. Everyone experiences it a little bit differently. Some people go through it very quickly, and are able to return to their lives. Your mom's just taking longer. We need to give her some time. We need to be patient. We just have to love her, even when she's not showing us love in return."

"But that's not *fair*, Dad! Why should I have to do that? She's my *mother*! She's supposed to love me! She's supposed to take me shopping, and look at my school work, and try to figure out which guy I like! But she doesn't do *any* of those things anymore. She's not my mother! She's a zombie!"

Dad takes a few deep breaths, staring at the table in front of him. Finally, he looks at me and says, "You're right, Kate. It's *not* fair. But sometimes life isn't fair. Right now, this is the hand we've been dealt, and we have to play the cards we've got. We can't just give up. Because the moment we give up, we lose."

"Okay, fine. I won't give up. I want the bead, Dad. I want it for Mom. I mean, what if it would help? What if that's the whole reason I found *my* bead?" My eyes plead with him. "Look, I don't want to take something away from a little girl who's sick. But Dad, don't you see? She's already better, and Mom isn't. Hannah's *already* got her miracle, but I still need one." The tears are flowing again and I wipe them away, angry with myself for being such an emotional basket case.

"Kate, it's true that a couple of pretty amazing coincidences have happened. But calling these things 'miracles' might be going a little far. Not everyone who's in a car accident dies, and medicine does cure people. I think you're placing way too much importance on a single little rosary bead."

"Maybe you're right, Dad. But it's all I've got. Getting that bead back is the only thing I can *do* to get Mom back. Please, Dad, I know you think it's all nonsense. I *know* you don't believe in any of it. I'm not even sure that I do. But we've come this far, and I don't think it's just a coincidence that we've found Mom's bead. Dad, I *can't* stop now. And if I have to buy my own plane ticket and fly to Florida to get that bead, I'll do it." I blurt the words out, not really thinking about what I'm saying.

Dad looks at me long and hard, without responding. The waitress arrives with our food, and we dig in, both relieved to have an excuse not to talk for a few minutes. About halfway through his tenderloin, Dad stops and says, "I'll tell you what, Kate. I think we could all use some time away. I'm not sure if your mother will go for it, but spring break is coming up. I'll talk it over with her. Maybe we can drive down to Florida, have a nice vacation, and go see Hannah and her family while we're—"

"*What?* Dad, that's awesome!" I squeal, jump from my seat and rush over to hug him. "Thank you, thank you, thank you!" I say, my arms still around his neck.

"Now, don't get your hopes up. I still need to discuss it with your mother, and I've got things I'll have to rearrange at the office. I promise that I'll try to make it work. But remember, Kate, even if we go down there, we're not going to just ask for your mom's bead back. We'll see what Hannah's family thinks, and we'll take things from there."

Properly chastised, I sit back down in my chair, but a smile continues to play at my lips. A vacation *and* a chance at getting Mom's bead back? I couldn't have asked for more.

It's Sunday morning, and I've been up since eight, watching TV, as I try to ignore a nagging desire to go to Mass. For the first fifteen years of my life, I spent most Sunday mornings complaining about being forced to attend the very thing that, for some unknown reason, I now want. Of all the crazy things. Yes, if I was really that set on the idea, I could ride my bike, or even walk, or ask Aunt Susan or Aunt Mary Ellen to come pick me up. But, the couch is comfy, and so are my pajamas, and the show's pretty funny. Perhaps next week I'll manufacture a sleepover at Evelyn's house, and then Mass will be a foregone conclusion.

Sometime later, my mind is slightly numb from sitcom reruns when I hear the phone ring. Gwen answers and brings it to Mom, who's reading a book in the sunroom.

"It's Aunt Mary Ellen," I hear Gwen tell Mom as she hands the phone over.

I try to focus on the television show, but have a hard time tuning out Mom's conversation.

"Mary Ellen, we just didn't feel like going today."

Pause. Mom closes the door to the sunroom. I get up and pretend to head toward the kitchen so I can listen from there.

"Well, you know, we can't all be perfect like you are, Mary Ellen." Her voice is muffled, but I can still hear it. "I've been going to Mass since the day I was born. Okay, so I missed a few during college, but I just haven't felt like going lately, and I don't know if I'll feel like going next Sunday either, or the Sunday after that, for that matter."

Pause. I think about Aunt Mary Ellen, who is super devout, goes to Mass every Sunday and most weekdays, goes to adoration, probably prays eighteen Rosaries a day, and used to be super close to my mom. I can't even imagine how she must feel, having this conversation with her big sister.

"You know, what does it really matter, 'what Mom would want?'" Mom practically spits out the words, anger dripping from her voice. "She's not here anymore. And besides, she went to Mass every Sunday, nearly every *day*, for that matter, and where'd it get her? She lost four babies, died in a terrible plane crash, and left us all here to pick up the pieces. You can say whatever you want, but I've never seen God, I've never felt God, he's never been there for me, and he *certainly* isn't here for me right now. So, you know what, Mary Ellen? I'm done!"

I stand stock still at my listening post. A few weeks ago, hearing Mom say she didn't want to go to Mass anymore would have filled me with glee, but now, surprisingly, I am brimming with despair. I knew Mom was struggling with her faith, but has it really come to *this*? Here I am, bent on finding these beads, and feeling more drawn to church, and Mom has decided to turn away from it completely.

I'm not going to cry. I've done enough of that lately. Too much. As I work to hold back the tears, Mom remains quiet, presumably listening to Mary Ellen. A few moments later, Mary Ellen must have said something to smooth things over, because I hear Mom say, "I love you, too." I creep away from the door, thinking about those words. I *love you*.

Those are good words. Words I certainly haven't heard her say in a while. Words I'd like to hear again.

Suddenly, I want nothing more than to see Aunt Mary Ellen, so I can talk to her and tell *her* about what's been going on. Quietly, I pad through the house, looking for the other cordless phone. Finding it, I go in my room and close the door.

I press the button for previous calls and, finding Aunt Mary Ellen's number, I push the "call" button.

Fourteen-year-old Thomas answers the phone. I hear him calling, "Mo-om, it's for you!" Then, a quizzical, "It's Kate," before Aunt Mary Ellen speaks into the phone.

"Kate?"

"Hi, Aunt Mary Ellen." Now, what to say? Somehow, I hadn't given it any thought, just picked up the phone and pressed the button.

"What's up?"

"Well, I overheard Mom talking to you a little bit ago, and I just wanted to talk to you. I don't really know why."

"That's okay, hon. You never need to have a reason to call me," she pauses. "We missed you at Mass today."

"Yeah, I actually kind of wanted to go for once, but, well…"

"How about I pick you up and we go to the evening Mass at St. Joan of Arc tonight? Maybe we can grab a bite to eat afterward?"

"Really? You'd do that? But you already went to Mass this morning!"

Aunt Mary Ellen chuckles. "There's nothing I'd rather do. Mass is always the highlight of my day. Going twice? Well, that's even better. I'll pick you up at four forty-five, okay? That'll give us plenty of time to pray a Rosary beforehand."

"Okay. That sounds good. I'll see you then." I hang up the phone and remove the necklace from around my neck, rolling the bead between my fingers for the thousandth time. Pray the Rosary with Aunt Mary Ellen? I remember the last time I prayed the Rosary, with Evelyn, and Mr. Billings called almost immediately after we finished. Could prayer really be so powerful? If I pray the Rosary today with Aunt Mary Ellen, will I get an immediate answer to my prayer again?

Funny, I had gone so long without praying much at all, let alone praying a whole Rosary, and now, I will have prayed two Rosaries in three days. I feel a little bit silly, spending so much time on something I never cared about before, and thinking that it will actually make a difference somehow. Yet, I find myself looking forward to seeing Aunt Mary Ellen, to praying with her, and to spending time with her after Mass.

Chapter Nine

I bite the bullet, summon my courage, and tell Mom that Aunt Mary Ellen is taking me to Mass and then dinner. Her face goes from stony to steel, but what is she going to do? Tell me, "No, Katelyn, you are not allowed to go to Mass?" Mom might have changed a lot in the past year, and she might have lost her faith, but apparently she's not so far gone that she'd tell me I can't go to Mass with her sister.

I spend some time agonizing over what I should wear. Aunt Mary Ellen's family is always more dressed up than ours for Mass, and I don't want to embarrass her when she's being so nice to me. Finally, I decide on a flowing blue skirt and lightweight white tunic, cinching a belt around the waist. The day is warm, so I throw on some sling-back sandals, grab my purse, and sit on the front porch to wait.

Aunt Mary Ellen pulls into the driveway a few minutes early, at 4:40. She shuts off the engine and walks toward the porch, her flowered skirt swinging as she walks.

"Hi, sweetie. How ya' doin'?" She presses me into a light hug before holding me at arms' length to peer into my face.

"Okay," I answer, looking away from her all-too-perceptive inspection.

"Is your mom home?"

"Um, yeah. I think she's in the kitchen." This could get interesting. I'm sure Mom doesn't want to see Mary Ellen right now.

"I'll just pop in and say a quick hello. Then we'll be on our way. Do you have your rosary?"

I fish it from my purse and hold it up for her to see.

"Great! Wait here, I'll be right back." And she disappears into the house, in search of her sister.

She returns a few moments later with a slightly strained look on her face. When she sees me looking at her, though, she offers a small smile. She ushers me to the car and we head to the church.

I've been to St. Joan of Arc a few times before, when we've missed morning Mass and had to come in the evening. As usual, I'm awed by the high, gothic ceilings, beautiful stained glass windows, and elegant statuary. We're a half hour early, so there are only a few other people in the pews, praying silently. Mary Ellen selects a pew near the front, kneels, and pulls out her rosary.

"What would you like us to pray for?" She asks in a whisper.

"My mom," I mumble back, a little uncomfortable.

"Okay. Shall I lead?" I nod, and she begins, quietly, so as not to disturb the others in the church. "In the name of the Father, and of the Son, and of the Holy Spirit."

I follow along better this time than I did when Evelyn and I prayed it on Friday. As Aunt Mary Ellen announces each mystery, I struggle to remember the story. The Resurrection I get, and the Ascension isn't so hard. The Descent of the Holy Spirit . . . isn't that where Peter goes out and talks to the crowd and they all hear him in their own language? As for the Assumption of the Blessed Virgin Mary and the Coronation, I am totally confused. I remember the May Crowning my eighth grade year, but all I can really think about is Ava Glasgow holding the flowery crown above the statue of Mary, and the cute little second grader holding the pillow, dressed in her beautiful First Communion dress.

"Pray for us, oh Holy Mother of God, that we may be worthy of the promises of Christ," Aunt Mary Ellen intones, and I come back to reality. Okay, so I haven't been totally focused, and I don't know all of the stories behind the mysteries, but nonetheless, I feel more peaceful and calm right now than I have since . . . well, since Evelyn and I prayed the Rosary two days ago.

As we make the Sign of the Cross, I look up at the crucifix in the front of the church, wishing that Jesus would just come down from there and explain all of this to me. How can praying on a bunch of beads do so much? Is it all just in my head? What do I do from here? Do I have to change and become a nun or something? Because that is *so* not going to happen.

I mean, seriously. Three weeks ago, I pretty much rolled my eyes at all this stuff. So why am I here, now, on a Sunday night when I didn't have to go to Mass, not only going to Mass, but praying a Rosary beforehand and actually *liking* it?

"No, thank you," Aunt Mary Ellen says, handing the wine menu back to the waiter. I raise my eyebrows, and Mary Ellen pulls a rueful smile. "I gave it up for Lent. Four more weeks and counting."

She orders water instead, and I ask for a root beer. We're at a place on 49th and Penn called Napolese Pizzeria where they make crazy pizzas with things like goat cheese and sweet potatoes on them. The adults always love it, but I prefer to stick to the basics. The Meridian Kessler pizza, named for the restaurant's Indianapolis neighborhood, sounds perfect—sausage, pepperoni, mushrooms, and good, old-fashioned mozzarella cheese—so I order that. Aunt Mary Ellen orders a salad.

As the waiter walks away, Aunt Mary Ellen sits back in her seat and takes a sip of water.

"So, Kate, tell me what's up."

The moment I've been waiting for, only I still have no idea what to say. I realize that she probably doesn't know anything about the beads, so I decide that that's a good place to start.

"Well, when we were at Grandma's memorial service, I found something," I begin.

"A bead?" Mary Ellen asks.

"Yes! How did you know?"

"Your Aunt Liz told me about it," she answers.

"Oh." That makes sense. I know they talk often.

"Do you have it with you? May I see it?" Mary Ellen asks. There's a certain pleading to her voice. She's held it together so well since Grandma died, it's easy to forget that she must really miss her too. Maybe it hasn't been as easy for her as I've imagined.

"I gave Aunt Liz's to Evelyn for now, but I have mine." I unfasten the necklace from around my neck and hand it to Mary Ellen. She holds it in her palm, rolling it around with the tip of her forefinger.

"I wish we had all of them. Wouldn't it be wonderful to be able to completely rebuild Mom's rosary?" she says, pensively.

"Well, I was kind of thinking that, if we could find more beads, it would be nice for each person to have their own," I say, suddenly unsure of myself.

Mary Ellen's hand closes around the bead, and a light sparks in her eyes. "You're right," she smiles. "That would be really wonderful. For each of us to have a little piece of something that was so special to your grandma." She hands the bead back to me a little reluctantly. "So, how has your mom handled you finding the two beads?"

"Well, it's not just two beads anymore. We've actually located five. But . . . we only *have* two of them. The other three are with a little girl in Florida who used to have cancer." I pause. "And Mom? Well, she's not taking it very well at all."

"What makes you think so? Has she done anything to stop you?"

I hesitate, not sure how to describe it. "Aunt Mary Ellen, Mom's been really different ever since Grandma died. She's been angry, and mopey, and totally not herself. It seems like nothing makes her happy. . . ." I wait a moment, struggling to say words that hurt so much, "Mom doesn't seem to like us anymore; she doesn't seem to want to be a *mom* anymore. It's like she's just trying to get through each day, wrapped up in her own little cocoon. And since she found out about the bead, she's been even more mad and more distant." I study my hands, and search for the right words. At a loss, the only thing left to say is, "It kind of stinks."

Aunt Mary Ellen reaches across the table and pats my folded hands. "Oh, Kate, I'm so sorry. I didn't know it had gone this far. This must be so difficult for you. And for Paul and Gwen, and your dad too. I'm afraid that I don't have any answers for you. But I miss the person she used to be, too. Perhaps we need to give your mom time to heal, time to find herself again."

Aunt Mary Ellen thinks for a moment. "Kate, I know you're young, and I don't expect that you'd think about this much, but have you been praying for your mom?"

I shrug my shoulders, uncomfortable. "No, not until today, I guess, when we prayed the Rosary."

"Do me a favor, Kate, okay? Every time you start to worry about your mom, every time you get mad at her, every time you resent her for how she's handling things, say a prayer for her. Can you do that? It can be a Hail Mary, or an Our Father, or something as simple as, 'Please, God, help my mom.' It doesn't really matter what you say, just pray. I'll be praying for her, too, Kate," she stretches her hands in front of her, grappling for the right words, "because the power of prayer is . . . well, it's amazing."

"I think I'm starting to get that. Some pretty crazy things have been happening." And I tell her the whole story—about finding the bead in the woods, meeting Chelsea and Emma, creating the flyer with Natalie, and her praying afterwards. Our food arrives as I'm telling her about praying the Rosary with Evelyn on Friday, and Mr. Billings calling right afterward. I explain about Roger Billings and his granddaughter, Hannah, between mouthfuls of pizza.

"So, what do you think, Aunt Mary Ellen?" I ask, hoping against hope that she has the answer. "I just don't get it. It can't all be a coincidence. It can't! But, if they're not coincidences, then what are they? Are these miracles?"

"Well, Kate, I don't have all the answers, but I do agree with you that these don't seem like random events. I'm a big believer in miracles, and I know that God is incredibly powerful, and will never cease to amaze us." I nod, as Mary Ellen pauses.

"You know who we ought to talk to about this?" she asks, then continues when I shake my head, "Your Uncle Joseph. I'm sure he could shed some light on the subject."

I nearly jump out of my seat. "Of course! Why didn't I think of that? He's sure to have answers!"

Aunt Mary Ellen gives me a wry smile, "Well, as much as it pains me to say that my little brother might know something I don't, I'll admit that he seems to have learned a thing or two in the seminary." I laugh, knowing as well as she does that Uncle Joseph is like a walking encyclopedia of biblical knowledge and Church doctrine. Looking at her watch, she continues, "Would you mind if I called him to see what he's up to? It's not too terribly late. We still have a little bit of time to pay him a visit."

When I agree, Aunt Mary Ellen fishes her phone out of her purse and places the call. A few minutes later, she ends the call and hands the phone to me.

"He said he'd meet us at that coffee shop downtown he likes. We just need to make sure it's okay with your parents."

I dial Dad's cell phone number, hoping he'll answer so I don't have to risk talking to Mom by calling the house. I breathe a sigh of relief when I hear his voice, and another when he says that it's fine for me to stay out a bit longer. Aunt Mary Ellen settles the bill and we hurry to the car.

When we arrive at the coffee shop, Uncle Joseph is already there, with drinks ready and waiting for us. We settle into our seats, and then, feeling like a broken record, I share the story of the beads one more time. He nods and murmurs, asking occasional questions, with Aunt Mary Ellen interjecting a missed detail here and there.

When I've finally finished, Uncle Joseph thinks for a few moments before beginning, "You know, Kate, your grandmother had a faith that I haven't seen in many people. We're never supposed to assume that someone's in heaven—or in hell for that matter, and I pray for Mom every day. But, if anyone I've known was going to make it to heaven, it was her. You know, growing up, I don't think I *ever* saw her lose her temper. She had seven kids, and yet—" He stops short when Aunt Mary Ellen lays a hand on his arms, a smile on her face.

"Oh, I remember one time, she came close! You were too young to remember this, Joseph, probably about two years old." She turns to me, "I was six years old. Dad was out of town on business, and Joseph was going through a phase where he refused to go to bed every night." She looks past me, into the coffee shop, clearly taking a trip down memory lane. "It was about eleven o'clock at night and she'd been going back and forth with him for hours. She had gone downstairs, thinking she finally had him in bed, but Joseph followed her down. I couldn't sleep because he was making so much noise, so I snuck down after him, and watched from the stairs. When she saw him walk into the kitchen, she went outside and sat down on a chair on the back porch. Joseph—of course—went to the back door, poked his head outside, and started crying again. 'Mommy! Mommy!'" Mary Ellen chuckles, her eyes clearly watching this scene play out in her mind's eye. "You know what Mom said?" She looks at Uncle Joseph, then at me, and laughs again. "You could hear in her voice that she was struggling to keep her cool." Mary Ellen lowers her voice, so that it's almost a growl, "'Joseph, go inside. I'm praying for patience.'" Raising her voice, Mary Ellen repeats, imitating Grandma so many years ago, "'I AM PRAYING FOR PATIENCE!'" She starts laughing again, her eyes twinkling as she looks at Joseph. "It's the closest I ever came to seeing her lose it."

Uncle Joseph laughs softly. "I can't say I remember that, but it does sum Mom up. She was *always* praying. Through thick and thin, good and bad, it was like she *breathed* prayer." He focuses his attention on me. "Kate, if anyone was going to heaven . . ."

He takes a deep breath. "Now, add to that the fact that she had an extremely strong devotion to the Blessed Virgin Mary. You remember her house? She had a crucifix above every door, and a statue of the Blessed Mother in every room."

Aunt Mary Ellen jumps in, "Some rooms had two, or even three!"

Nodding his head, Uncle Joseph continues, "She didn't talk about it much, but she would pray while she folded clothes, cooked dinners, and swept the floors. I remember walking into the bathroom once. Mom was down on her knees, reaching around to scrub the back of the toilet, and under her breath, guess what she was saying?" He looks at Mary Ellen, who pounds on the table as they both say,

"Hail Mary, full of grace!"

They both laugh, and I find myself joining in as I imagine my dignified grandma scrubbing toilets while praying the Rosary.

Uncle Joseph sobers a bit and leans forward in his chair. "When he was dying on the cross, Jesus said 'I thirst.' Now, why do you think he said that?"

"Um . . ." I shrug and answer, "Because he needed some water?"

Uncle Joseph smiles, "Well, yes, I'm sure he did, but those words hold an even deeper meaning. Christ thirsted for *souls*. He wanted people to come to him, and—through him—to his Father." He pauses, letting that soak in for a moment, then continues, "Do you know what Christ had said just before he spoke those words?" He raises his eyebrows, waiting for me to respond, but I shake my head.

Uncle Joseph turns and looks at Aunt Mary Ellen, who answers his question, "Was it, 'Woman, behold your son!' and, to John, 'Behold, your mother!'?"

"Yes! Exactly," he smiles and turns back to me. "Jesus gave his mother Mary to the disciple John. He wanted them to think of each other as mother and son. But it was a lot bigger than that." He takes a sip of his coffee as I nod obedi-ently, though I'm not really sure where he's going with this. "What Jesus was doing," Uncle Joseph continues, "was giving Mary to the *world* as our mother, and giving *all of us* to Mary as her children. I like to think that those two statements are related. Jesus longs for souls, and he's giving all of humanity to his mother as her children, asking her to help quench that longing."

Uncle Joseph has been creeping further and further up in his seat as he talks, and now he finally leans back, relaxed. "Kate, I've spent a lot of time thinking about that. It's one of my favorite things to ponder when I pray the mystery of the Crucifixion. And I *always* get chills when I think about it."

He sits forward eagerly again. "So, you see, Kate, the Blessed Mother's number one job is to *bring souls to Christ*, and she's up there in heaven, doing just that—doing every-thing she possibly can to bring more people to know and love Jesus. So, when someone like your grandma, who loved Mary *so* much, and who was led to Jesus *through* Mary, dies . . . well, I figure that Mary and Mom are working together to bring everyone in this family closer to Christ. I've felt their work in my own life, and I believe that's what's happening in yours."

Joseph picks up the bead, which I had placed on the table when I first started sharing my story. "All these things that have happened . . . a voice at a car accident, a healing from cancer . . . Do I think they're miracles?" He looks me deep in the eyes.

"Well, Kate, 'nothing is impossible with God. . . .'" A smile lights his face, and he leans back in his chair again. The smile slowly spreads, brightening his eyes, "And I can't wait to see what more he has in store for us!"

Chapter Ten

It's late when we finally leave the coffee shop, and we drive home under the streetlights with the heater blasting. I walk up the front steps after Aunt Mary Ellen drops me off, feeling buoyed by our conversation with Uncle Joseph.

The house is quiet, and it appears as though everyone has already gone to bed. I groan as I realize that I've still got homework to do. Resigning myself to a late night, I go into the kitchen to grab a glass of water before I head upstairs. The stark white of a note on the black granite countertop catches my attention, and I pause to read it.

K—*Chelsea called. Says she has news.*—Dad

My heart leaps. I'll bet someone else has a bead! A quick glance at the clock assures me that it's way too late to call, and I smack the note back down on the counter in frustration. It will have to wait until tomorrow.

I grab the note and carry it upstairs, needing the reassurance that I haven't just imagined it in a delusional late night fog. I settle into my history book, trying to make sense out of words that swim before my tired eyes, while my mind buzzes with thoughts of beads, miracles, and two women up to all sorts of heavenly mischief.

I wake the following morning lying fully clothed on top of my bedspread. As I drowsily swing my legs to the floor, I glance at my desk to find that my history book is still open to the same page I started on last night, and I've written three numbers on my timeline of World War II. Clearly, the year 193 does not play a significant role in twentieth-century war. I groan, look at the clock, which reads 7:10, and have no choice but to close my book and shove it in my backpack. My first late assignment all year. I jerk the zipper closed and head to the bathroom to freshen up before school.

When I race into the kitchen, Dad's standing at the island, dressed and ready for work.

"Grab something to eat and hop in the car," he says. "I'm taking you to school today."

"Where's Mom?" I ask.

"In bed. She's not feeling well."

I shrug, grab a banana, and head out the door for Dad's car. As we drive toward the school, though, I think about how unusual it is for Mom to sleep in. I don't think I've seen her in bed after sunrise more than five times in my entire life.

I immediately look for Evelyn when I get to school, and see that she's standing by her locker talking to our friend, Morgan. We haven't told anyone at school about finding Grandma's rosary beads, and I'm hesitant to bring the subject up now, in front of someone else. I say hi to them both, and give Evelyn a look that I hope says, "I need to talk to you," then go to my locker and start unloading my backpack. As I'm gathering the books for my first two classes, Evelyn appears at my side.

"What's up?" she whispers loudly.

"Chelsea called. There's news." I answer.

Evelyn gives a small squeal and claps her hands excitedly. "Eeee! What is it?"

"I don't know. I wasn't home. Dad took the message."

"You didn't call her back?" Evelyn asks incredulously.

"No, it was too late when I got home, and, of course, it was too early to call her this morning."

"How's it happen you were out late on a Sunday night?"

"I went to evening Mass at St. Joan of Arc with Aunt Mary Ellen, and then we went out for dinner at Napolese. I told her about everything that's been going on, and we ended up meeting Uncle Joseph so he could weigh in on the subject."

Evelyn's brows arch up, and I know she has more questions, but the bell rings, signaling that it's time to get to class.

"Come to my house after school. We can call her back from there." Evelyn says as we walk quickly down the hall.

"That'd be great, as long as my mom says it's okay." I'd much rather call Chelsea from friendly territory, where I won't have to worry about Mom overhearing me.

We take our seats and quiet down just in time for the final bell to ring.

⁂

When I see Mom in the car line, I'm startled by the dark circles under her eyes, and the way that she's slouched behind the wheel of the car. Gwen and Paul sit in the back-seat, their faces reflecting my own concern.

"Are you okay? You look terrible!" I blurt out, and then cover my mouth, shocked at my thoughtless words.

She doesn't look at me, just shakes her head and waves her hand for me to get in the car.

"Actually, Evelyn asked me to come to her house this afternoon," I say, awkwardly, "but if you need me to drive, or anything . . ."

"No. Go to Evelyn's," she says, her voice sounding funny. I hesitate, and she urges, "*Please*, go to Evelyn's."

And I realize . . . *she doesn't want me to come home.*

My emotions war with each other as I walk with Evelyn. On the one hand, I'm very happy to be going to her house, and happy to be able to call Chelsea from there, where I don't risk offending or upsetting Mom. I'm also happy to be away from the dour atmosphere of our home for a few hours. On the other hand, my feelings are hurt that my own mother doesn't want me around. What have I done to make her dislike me *that much*? My emotions swing from an angry desire to just keep doing more of *whatever* it is that's bothering her, and a keen longing to do whatever it would take to make her love me again.

Evelyn chatters away all the way home. There's a guy she likes in our class, so she fills me in on all the latest and greatest about *Mitchell*. What he was wearing today, the color of his eyes, the fact that he said hello this morning and asked her if she liked the pizza at lunch. It's pretty easy to tune her out, mumble the occasional "mm-hmmm" and "Really?" and pretend that I'm listening, all while struggling with the gazillion thoughts thundering through my head. Yet, by the time we reach Evelyn's house, I'm no closer to an answer about much of anything. One thing I know: I can't undo the whole bead thing, and I wouldn't really want to, even if I could. And I'm not going to stop searching for the other beads, either. Mom's just going to have to deal with it!

We enter the house through the back door, and swing through the kitchen for a snack, saying a quick hello to Aunt Susan. We tell her that Chelsea has news for us, and head upstairs to make the phone call.

I try the restaurant, but they say she's not working today. I call her cell, but she doesn't answer. So, I leave a message, and Evelyn and I start working on our homework while we wait for the return phone call. Finally, an hour later, the phone rings. We recognize the caller ID immediately.

"Hello? Chelsea?"

"Hi! Yeah, it's me. Sorry I missed your call. I was still at school," she responds. "So, you got my message?"

"Yeah. What's up?"

"Well, a woman came into the restaurant yesterday, and I noticed her reading the flyer. She stood by the door looking at it for a really long time, and I finally went over and asked her if I could help her with something. She said that she didn't need anything, but had just seen the flyer and wasn't sure what to do. Apparently, she found one of the beads last year, but doesn't have it anymore."

My whoop of excitement dies in my throat as Chelsea finishes the sentence. "She doesn't have it anymore?" I repeat, "What happened to it?"

"Well, I'm not sure. She started to tell me, and was saying something about her brother, but then she looked at her watch and said she was late getting back to work. She gave me her card, and I said I'd have you call her."

Chelsea gives me the woman's name and number, and we chat for a few minutes. I tell her about Mr. Billings and his granddaughter, Hannah, and her seemingly miraculous recovery.

"Wow, Kate. First Emma was saved in that car accident. Now, this little girl is, like, cured of cancer? I wonder what else you're going to find," Chelsea muses.

"Yeah, pretty amazing, huh? Look, I want to call this lady before she leaves work for the day. I'll let you know what she says, okay?"

I hang up. Evelyn's been listening with her ear plastered next to mine, so there's no need to fill her in. I immediately dial the woman's number, knowing that if I stop to think about it I'll get nervous.

Nonetheless, my heart is pounding when the call is answered on the second ring. "Hendricks Pediatrics. This is Beth. How may I help you?"

"Uh, hi," I fumble. "Um, my name is Katelyn Roberts. I understand you found a bead that I'm looking for?"

"Oh, yes! Hi, Katelyn. Yes, I did find a bead. I found it on the side of the road one day—oh, seven or eight months ago, I guess—when I was out walking my dog. I'm afraid I don't have it anymore, though."

Even though Chelsea had already said this, I feel my heart sink as I hear the words come down the phone line. "Yeah, that's what Chelsea—the girl at the restaurant—said. Do you know where it is?"

"Well, sort of." She takes a deep breath, as if she's collecting her thoughts. I adjust the phone, trying to hold it so Evelyn can hear as well. Beth continues, "My little brother—well, he's forty-two," she chuckles. "Geesh, when did we get so old? Anyway, my brother, James . . ."

She hesitates for long enough to make me wonder if the call dropped.

"Well, to make a long story short," she continues, "James is homeless, and lives in a tent community downtown. He's addicted to goodness-only-knows-what, but every once in a while, he sobers up enough to call me from a pay phone, and we usually set up a time and place to meet.

"Oddly enough, that bead I found had his initials on it, J C L. Even stranger, he called right after I got home from walking the dog that day."

Evelyn gasps at this, and I clench the phone as shivers run down my arms. The woman continues, "He sounded terrible, and I was anxious to see him. We set up a time to meet the next day. I brought him that bead because it had his initials on it. It just seemed like it was meant for him. I feel terrible now, though. I'm sorry."

When she pauses, I glance at Evelyn, unsure of how to respond. Before I can formulate any words, though, Beth rushes on, "Chances are, he's pawned it, or traded it for drugs, so I doubt I can get it back for you. The other problem is that I haven't heard from him since." I hear her take a deep breath and let it out in a sad sigh. "This is the longest James has ever gone without calling me. I keep thinking the next I'll hear of him will be from the police, or a story in the news about a dead homeless man." Beth gives a soft, sad laugh.

I'm at a total loss for words, and just hang on to the other end of the line awkwardly. Beth clears her throat and says, "So, that's the story. Give me your number, and I'll let you know if I hear from him. If he does call, I'll be sure to ask about the bead, and I promise to get it back for you if I can."

I give Beth the phone number, mumble something about how sure I am that her brother is fine, and hang up the phone before sinking down onto the bed, deflated.

Evelyn sits down too, and puts her arm around me. "There will be other beads, Kate."

"I know. It's just . . . you know, the two people who have seen the flyers don't even have the beads anymore. It seems like we're getting nowhere with this."

"We'll find more beads, Kate," Evelyn says adamantly. "Don't give up. All of this is happening for a reason. I just know it is!" Evelyn stops and it's clear that she's had a revelation.

"Hey, have you still been praying?" she asks.

I look at her a bit guiltily. "No. I forgot."

"I confess. I did too. But it's never too late to start again. I have to get going soon for practice, but I could call you later and we could pray a Rosary over the phone?"

"Seriously? Isn't that a little *weird*?"

"Well, I don't see why it would be. Besides, I've heard my mom do it with one of her friends from church."

"Okay, as long as I've got my history done. I fell asleep last night and didn't finish it."

"Uh oh. Did ol' Mrs. Perkins put the smackdown on you?"

"No, not too bad. It's the first time all year, so she was pretty cool about it. But if it's not done tomorrow..."

"Say no more. If you're not done we'll just do it tomorrow instead."

Evelyn is exhibiting a streak of determination that I didn't know she had. Sure, she's determined in softball and cross country, and in her school work and things like that. But this insistence on prayer is a totally new thing for me to see. Apparently, all of the strange things that have been going on are getting to her, too.

Chapter Eleven

Thirty minutes later, I walk into my house to find Paul and Gwen sitting on the couch watching television, with the volume so low I can barely hear it.

"Hey, guys! What's up?" I ask.

They both start as if they've heard a gunshot. Gwen puts a finger to her lips and shushes me, while Paul admonishes me in a loud whisper, "Quiet! Don't bother Mom!"

I look at both of them quizzically, then sit down in the chair by the couch.

"What's going on?" I whisper.

"I don't know. Something's wrong with Mom. She went straight to her room when we got home from school, and she's been there ever since. If we make *any* noise, she yells at us to be quiet," Paul answers.

Just then I hear the whine of the dog.

"Where's Amber?" I ask.

"We had to put her in her crate. She kept scratching at Mom's door, and Mom was getting really upset."

As the oldest in the family, I figure it's my job to find out what's up. Cautiously, I tiptoe up the stairs and down the hall toward Mom and Dad's bedroom, wincing with every creak of the wooden floor boards.

I knock quietly on the door, then carefully unlatch it and push it open a few inches.

"Mom?" I say quietly, peering into the dark room. The blinds are drawn, blocking out the sunlight, and I can just make out the outline of her body lying on the bed beneath the covers. "Are you okay?"

Mom pulls the pillow over her head. "I'm fine. Just leave me alone."

I stand there for a moment, unsure of what to do. Clearly, she is *not* "fine." Just as clearly, she does not want to be disturbed. I close the door with a soft *click* and tiptoe back downstairs.

I start to grab my backpack so that I can finish my homework, but then my stomach growls and I realize that it will be dinnertime soon, and Mom hasn't started anything.

The price of being the oldest, I think, as I look longingly to the couch where Paul and Gwen are still sitting. Homework will wait. Right now, somebody needs to cook dinner.

I look through the fridge and cupboards to try to figure out something I actually know how to make. There's mac-n-cheese, salad mix, tomato soup, a loaf of bread . . . I check the fridge for cheese slices and finally settle on grilled cheese sandwiches with tomato soup. Not a gourmet meal, but—hey—I'm sixteen years old, and it'll have to do. At least I will have tried. If all else fails, maybe we can order pizza once Dad gets home.

He arrives as I'm doing a final flip of the grilled cheese sandwiches on the oversized electric skillet. The table is set and I've even thought to put some grapes in a bowl. All in all, I'm pretty pleased with myself. However, when Dad walks through the door and sees me fixing dinner, he runs a hand through his hair, looking worried.

"How's your mom?" He asks.

"She's upstairs in bed," I answer. "Is she sick or something? She looked awful."

"I'm not sure, honey," he sits down heavily in a chair, looking as though he bears the weight of the world, "but I'm afraid . . . well, I'm afraid that losing Grandma might have been more than she could handle."

"That doesn't make any sense, though," I protest. "Sure, Mom's changed since Grandma died, but she didn't stay in bed all day like this when it first happened. Why would she get worse *now*, a year later?"

"I know it's hard to understand, Kate. I think . . ." He rests his forehead on his clasped hands for a moment before looking back up at me. "I think she was able to hold it together for a while, but going to the crash site, and—well—everything else that's happened were just more than she could bear."

I stare at him as I digest his words. *Everything else that's happened*. He means the beads. I'm not sure whether I feel guilty or angry, or both, and I'm definitely not sure how I should respond. So, I turn back to the electric skillet to rescue the sandwiches before they burn. Through a blur of tears and with a strangled voice, I ask Dad to tell the others that dinner's ready.

I hear his chair scoot back and a moment later feel the warmth of his hand as he squeezes my shoulder.

"We'll figure something out, Kate. It'll be okay," he says, then leaves the room to check on Mom before calling Gwen and Paul to the table.

Dinner is a quiet affair, though the food is surprisingly good. It's just four of us, since Mom said she didn't want to eat. Dad makes a few attempts to lighten the mood, but it's clear that we're all worried about Mom. Afterward, Dad gives me a hug and thanks me for cooking.

"You go upstairs and finish your homework. We'll take care of the dishes."

I look gratefully around the kitchen, taking in the disaster I managed to create in preparing a relatively simple meal. I smile a thank you to Dad, before walking quietly up to my room. Mom's door is still closed, and there's no light coming from underneath.

I typically like history, but tonight World War II holds no interest for me as I attempt to finish the timeline that should have been done this morning. Between concern for what's going on with Mom, and thinking about Beth and her brother James, I'm too distracted. I can't stop wondering if we'll be able to get Mom's bead from Hannah, and whether anyone else will ever call about any of the other beads.

At eight thirty, the phone rings. I pounce on it, horrified that Mom might be disturbed. It's Evelyn, wanting to pray the Rosary together. I groan inwardly. I have been staring at this timeline for an hour and have only written three dates on it. I've still got algebra homework to do, as well. The last thing I need to spend time on right now is a twenty-minute prayer.

Evelyn jumps right in. "Hey! Are you done with your homework?"

"No. I've got a long way to go."

"Okay. We'll be quick. Fifteen minutes. I promise."

"Seriously, Ev. I can't focus on my homework. There's a lot going on. I really can't do this right now."

"No, Kate, that's exactly why you need to do this. How did you feel after we prayed on Friday?"

"Better," I admit grudgingly.

"And, you went to Mass with Aunt Mary Ellen last night, so I'm willing to bet you prayed a Rosary with her before-hand, right?"

"Yes." I give another grudging reply.

"And how did you feel after that?" Evelyn asks in a smug tone. She clearly already knows the answer.

"Better. But I was praying for something else, and we were in a church, we weren't doing it over the phone. This seems silly, and I've got a gazillion things to do, and I'm *tired* and I want to go to bed." I hear the whine in my voice, but choose to ignore it.

"Sorry," she says, "but I'm sticking to my guns. In the name of the Father, and of the Son, and of the Holy Spirit. Amen. I believe . . ."

I sit there with my mouth gaping open, shocked at how pushy she's being, while realizing that my right hand is making the Sign of the Cross of its own accord. I seriously consider hanging up, but that seems totally sacrilegious— and pretty rude. Meanwhile, as I battle myself internally —pray, hang up, pray, hang up, pray, hang up—Evelyn is zipping through the Rosary at warp speed. She's saying it so fast that I can barely make the words out.

Does this even count?

Next thing I know, we're already on the second mystery, and I don't even know what set of mysteries we're supposed to be praying today . . . the ones about Jesus' birth? His death? I'm totally lost!

"HailMaryfullofgracetheLordiswiththee." Okay, I've caught on enough, and I feel like an auctioneer but here goes:

"HolyMaryMotherofGodprayforussinnersnowandatthe- hourofourdeath." Whew! I'm breathless. Okay, again!

I finally catch the mystery when Evelyn states the next one. The Nativity. Okay. I can remember that story. Jesus. Born. Stable. Shepherds. Wise men. Got it.

Then it's on to the Presentation—not so sure about that one; then Jesus Found at the Temple. I think I remember a thing or two about that and then, before I know it, Evelyn's finishing with a flourish. I find that I've sunk to my knees and am kneeling at my bedside and . . . lo and behold, once the dust settles and I can find my breath again, I actually do feel better.

Huh.

"Okay! That's it! This is Evelyn Langford, signing off. Now go finish your homework. See you tomorrow!" She makes a loud smacking-kiss sound, chuckles, and—*click*—the line is dead.

I stand up, sit down at my desk, and finish the timeline in twenty minutes. The algebra's a breeze, and before I know it I'm tucked into bed. Dad comes and gives me a hug and kiss goodnight, and I'm out like a light.

Evelyn puts so much faith in prayer, that I wake the next morning feeling confident that things will be all better. Yet, when I come down for breakfast, Mom's nowhere to be seen and it's clear that Dad is on duty again. I don't bother asking this time. I'm sure the answer will be the same: "Your mom's not feeling well."

I half expect the phone to ring before we even leave for school, even though it's crazy early. After all, the last time Evelyn and I prayed for someone to call, they did, and within minutes.

Three days later, no one's called, and you can imagine my disappointment. Add to that the fact that Mom's still holed up in her room with the blinds closed, and I'm ready to throw my rosary out the window. It clearly isn't working.

Thinking that perhaps Aunt Mary Ellen can shine some light on this subject, I pick up the phone. Then I decide that she'll just tell me to pray so I hang it back up. I think about what Uncle Joseph said on Sunday night and I pick up the phone again. Then I realize that I don't really feel like hearing any "wisdom" right now. I just want Mom out of her bedroom, and five calls from people who have found beads, so I hang it back up. This time, to remove the temptation to call my aunt, I head downstairs to make dinner. Yet again.

Tonight I'm feeling ambitious, and I want to drown out thoughts of Mom, rosaries, and calling Aunt Mary Ellen. Besides, I think everyone's had enough macaroni and cheese and grilled cheese sandwiches to last a lifetime. I pull out Mom's recipe book and decide to make a family favorite, Johnny Marzetti. This is one of those recipes Mom used to make often, so locating the ingredients is pretty easy. The hamburger and sausage are in the freezer, and I defrost them in the microwave before putting them in the skillet. There's one onion and half a green pepper left in the fridge. I chop those and leave them to sit as I brown the meat. I boil water and add rotini pasta to it, then lose myself in the mundane task of pushing meat around a skillet.

As I work, I remember the times when I used to help Mom in the kitchen. For as long as I can remember, she's let me stir and measure. She started letting me use the sharp knives when I was eight. I remember feeling so grown up, standing at the counter on a stool to chop an onion, and being so embarrassed when tears ran down my face and I didn't even know why. Mom laughed and gave me a hug and said, "Sweetheart, chopping onions makes everyone cry— even me! Here, let me show you." She took the knife from me, and before I knew it, she, too, was sniffling and wiping her eyes with the corner of her chic apron. She looked up from the onion, gave me a wide smile, and said, "See?" Then she bent down and started tickling me and I tried to tickle her back. We both collapsed on the floor in a fit of giggling.

The memory makes me smile, thinking about how it used to be. She was a really good mom. Whoever would have thought that she could change into this . . . this shadow of the mother that she once was. And, these past few days, she hasn't even been a shadow—more like an empty void.

Now I find myself crying again, and it has nothing to do with onion. Something's got to give. We can't continue to live like this, and I'm beginning to really worry about Mom. I haven't seen her eat anything in days. I sneak into her room after school each day and bring her a little something—a bagel, an apple, anything I think she might enjoy, but she never takes more than a bite or two. Maybe tomorrow I'll ask Dad to stop and get her some frozen yogurt—vanilla and orange cream swirl, with her favorite toppings. How can she survive, barely eating?

I haven't asked Dad about that trip down to visit Hannah, but I've decided to talk to him tonight. Some warm air and sunshine would do all of us good, especially Mom. She clearly needs to step foot outside of her bedroom again, although I'm not sure she'd be willing to go at this point. But the more I think about it, the more I believe Hannah and her family might be willing to give us the bead, now that Hannah's better. The beads seem to have worked miracles for Emma and Hannah. Surely they could make a difference for Mom?

I shake myself out of my reverie, and, upon assuring myself that the meat is sufficiently cooked, add the onion and green pepper. Finally, it's all ready to combine into the casserole dish and top with cheese. I forgot to preheat the oven, so I read for a bit while waiting for it to heat, then throw my creation in when a *ding* tells me the oven is ready. I stand back and survey the kitchen, which has now become my domain, feeling pleased with myself, despite all of my worry over Mom. I haven't even made too much of a mess, and if the meal is anywhere near as good as it smells, we're all in for a treat.

A half hour later, I pull dinner from the oven and place it on the table, then call the family to dinner with a flourish, proud of my accomplishment.

Gwen and Paul dig in and eat with gusto, but Dad just picks at his food and barely eats a bite. A few minutes later, Gwen asks, "Where's the fruit?"

I glance around the table and realize that I was so busy fixing the casserole, and thinking about Mom, that I forgot to fix anything *but* the casserole. I start to get up, but Dad puts a hand on my shoulder and tells me he'll get it.

A few minutes later, with canned peaches added to the table, I notice that Dad still isn't eating, and he glances around at the three of us. Gwen and Paul are devouring the fruit, as I sit staring back at Dad. He clears his throat, straightens in his chair, and then folds his hands on the table in front of him.

"Kids, I need to talk to you about . . ." he clears his throat again, "about your mom."

He looks at each of us, making sure that we're all paying attention.

"Well, guys, your mom's . . . well . . . she's not *well*."

The woman hasn't come out of her room in four days. Not *well* seems like a bit of an understatement.

"Yeah, Dad, we know." Paul says, quietly.

"I think . . . I think she needs some help." He rubs his hand over his eyes, and I suddenly realize how tired he looks. "I've talked with a friend of mine who's a psychologist, and he recommended that we get some counseling for her. What she's doing right now . . . not eating, staying in bed all day. . . well, he says that there is . . . there's cause for concern, and that it might be best for her to go to a . . ."—he clears his throat—"a wellness center for a . . . a few weeks." Dad, usually so well spoken, stumbles over the words.

Dad leans both elbows on the table in front of him and buries his face in his hands, pressing his fingers into the corners of his eyes as if to stop the tears from coming. When he lifts his face, I can see that he was not successful. His fingers are wet, and now the tears are streaking down his cheeks.

"I talked with her this afternoon, and she's agreed. She . . ." —he looks around the table at us again, like he's trying to reassure us—"she knows that something's wrong, and she doesn't want to be this way either. She just doesn't know how to come out of it." He pauses, takes a deep breath, and continues, "I found a good place, one that comes highly recommended by my friend. He says she'll be comfortable there and that they are very successful in helping people, especially people dealing with depression and grief. I'll be taking her there tomorrow, after you're at school."

I feel a rush of mixed emotions as Dad explains this. First, there's a guilty sense of relief. Life with Mom in the house has become pretty miserable. Sneaking around, trying not to make a peep or step an inch out of line: it's awful. The thought of being able to actually live in our house again makes me more than just a little bit happy.

But then there's also a terrible sadness. I can't believe that my mom is checking into some sort of mental health facility. She's supposed to be stronger than that. She's supposed to be the one I rely on. She's supposed to be there for me when I cry, and when I celebrate, and when I laugh. Sure, she hasn't been *that person* for a year now, but this makes her decline much more real to me.

The third emotion is one I'm not proud to confess: embarrassment. How am I going to explain to everyone that my mom has suddenly disappeared? "Oh, yeah, my mom checked into the loony bin," or "A darkened room was no longer enough, so we got her a padded cell"? I find myself dreaming up excuses, distortions of the truth like, "Oh, Mom needed a break so she's going on her own little vacation."

Fourth? I'm ticked. Ticked that I prayed for her with Aunt Mary Ellen, and then I prayed again Monday night with Evelyn, and even if the intention then wasn't *for* Mom, surely it should count for something? Surely it should have *helped*? But it didn't. She's worse, and this situation is worse, and I want it to just be over, but I see no end in sight. So, what's the use in praying if this is all you get in return? Why bother? I'm starting to think that life was better before all of this started to happen—before I found the bead, before I heard the amazing stories, before we started on this search. Life was *better* when I hadn't prayed a darn Rosary in eight years!

Paul and Gwen are asking questions, but I don't want to hear the answers. I push my chair away from the table and stand up abruptly. "I'm not hungry anymore," I say before nearly running up the stairs to the privacy of my room.

Once there, I give my pillow a few good punches, but that doesn't make me feel better, so I throw the pillow across the room. Another pillow follows, then another, and another. One of the pillows knocks over a ballerina figurine on my dresser that Grandma gave me when I was four. It smashes to the floor and breaks into tiny pieces. I try to catch it, but of course I'm too late. Tears stream down my face as I pick up the pieces of porcelain. I hold them in my hand and wonder, *Why? Why is this happening to me? What have I done to deserve this?*

I throw the pieces, one by one, into the trash can, each one making a satisfying *donk!* as it hits the metal can, all the while thinking, *It must be me. I must have made all this happen. I was mean to Gwen, and I disrespected Mom all the time. I didn't help out enough around the house.* Finally, the pieces are gone, the sobs rip from my body, and I vow—to whoever might be listening—"I'll do better! I'll *be* better! I promise, I will. I *promise.* Just bring her back. Bring me back my mom." I continue to mumble my demand as I curl in a ball on the floor, my arms wrapped around my knees, wishing for comfort but finding none.

A little while later, Dad opens the door softly and finds me lying on the floor, my sobs reduced to dry hiccups. He sits down next to me and gathers me into his arms. I wish I was a little girl again so he could pick me up, carry me to my bed, cover me in my blankets and give me a hug that never ends. But I'm not, so I settle for this, on the hard floor, with my daddy gently rocking back and forth, cradled in the warm strength of his arms, his heartbeat under my ear drowned out occasionally by a hiccup from my residual cries.

For a long time, he doesn't say anything, and I'm glad. Words would ruin the solace that his warmth gives. He simply rocks me, periodically smoothing my hair back from my forehead or rubbing my arm in a comforting gesture.

Finally, the hiccups are gone and I begin to feel silly being held in my father's arms like this. I move to get up, but he doesn't let me go.

"Kate, I know this is hard. Probably harder on you than it is on Paul and Gwen. I'm sorry that you have to go through this, sorry for everything that's happened in the last year, and I wish I could just make it all go away for you. But I can't." His arms tighten around me, "Mom is going to get better, but it isn't going to happen overnight. We've just got to stick together and get through this."

He finally lets me go, and I sit up but don't look him in the eye. "How long will she be there?" I ask.

"It'll depend on how long it takes them to stabilize her. Probably a few weeks, then she'll be able to come home and do outpatient treatment."

"Can we go visit her?" I ask, but I'm not sure that I'll really want to.

"I'm not sure, honey. We'll know more after tomorrow."

"So I guess this means we're not going to Florida to see Hannah over spring break?" I finally sneak a glance at him, and I can see that he's been crying too.

"No, sweetie, we can't leave your mom right now, and she's not up for traveling. Maybe in the summer, okay?"

"But, Dad, what if the bead could help her? Aunt Elizabeth's bead helped Emma, and the other beads helped Hannah. What if *that's* what Mom needs, Dad?"

"Kate, we talked about this before. A bead does not hold some magical power. There's no such thing as magic, honey. You know that."

"I didn't say it was *magic*, Dad. But what if it's some special link to Grandma? What if Grandma's praying for the people who have her beads?"

Dad's clearly uncomfortable with the direction of the conversation, and anxious to put an end to it. "Kate, if there is a heaven, your grandmother would be there. But I'm not sure how much she could do from there. And, if she *could* make things happen, I can't imagine why she would need a bead to do it."

He stands up, brushing his pants as he does. "Look, you know I'm not the right person to talk to about this. I'm sure your Uncle Joseph could help, or even Aunt Susan or Mary Ellen." He holds a hand out to help me up. I take it, and he pulls me to my feet and into another hug. I draw comfort from his warmth, a father's combination of strength and softness, and I relax in his arms for a moment. He rests his chin on the top of my head.

"Kate, I love you so much. We're gonna get through this, baby. We'll get through it together. Okay?"

The tears start to come again, but I hold them back. I nod my head, chin wobbling, and pull gently from his embrace, looking at my feet. "Okay, Dad," I manage in a strangled voice.

Anxious now for this conversation to be over, I look at my desk, where my history book lies open, waiting for me to study for the test over World War II. "I'd better get my homework done," I mumble, then walk to my desk and sit on the chair. I simply can't face him right now.

He walks up behind me, gives my shoulder a gentle squeeze, and says, "Okay, sweetie. Can I get you anything?"

I shake my head, afraid that I'll start to cry again if I try to speak. Dad gives me a kiss on the crown of my head, and then quietly leaves the room, closing the door behind him.

Chapter Twelve

The house is eerily quiet the following morning. No one quibbles over who gets the first shower, and Gwen doesn't ask if she can borrow any of my clothes for today's casual day. Everyone gets their own breakfast and we eat in silence. What do you talk about on the morning that your mom's headed to a mental hospital? Exactly. Nothing. There's really nothing to say.

I struggle with what to tell Evelyn, and when. She'll find out eventually—sooner, rather than later, I'm sure, being family and all. Plus, she's my best friend, and I know I ought to *want* to tell her. But that crushing embarrassment continues to plague me. There's just no way to feel *good* about your mom going to a "facility." Oh, sure, Dad tries to make it sound nice by calling it a "wellness center," but we all know the truth.

I sneak a glance at Gwen, then Paul, and I can see that they all slept about as well as I did. They look awful, and I know that I do too. My eyes are red rimmed and puffy, my cheeks stained from the tears that coursed down them on and off throughout the night. The lack of sleep added dark circles to the mix, and I'm more than a little mortified by the thought of facing everyone at school. I think of all of us Roberts pulling up to the school together, looking like death warmed over, and find that my mouth actually curves into a small smile as I compare us to the vampire family from the *Twilight* series. For a moment, I simply enjoy the fact that I can still smile, before reality sets in and the smile disappears.

Dad arrives in the kitchen, ready to take us to our respective schools. He looks awful too. He places a mug on the coffee machine, puts a cup in the dispenser, and presses the button. Moments later, he leans against the granite countertop, closes his eyes, and breathes in the aroma of the dark roast, as if it holds the key to his well-being. When he opens his eyes, though, they're anxious, and I can see that he is dreading what this day will bring.

He glances at the clock. "Time to go, guys. Do you want to go up and say bye to Mom?"

The three of us look at each other, a little startled. Somehow, the thought doesn't seem to have occurred to any of us. I'm filled with dismay. What would I say? What will Mom do? I can't possibly imagine a more awkward situation, but I know that I have a duty, as the oldest, to lead the way. I straighten my shoulders, give a quick, slightly jerky nod of my head, and resolutely head for the stairs.

We only have a few minutes, a mercy for which I think I'll be eternally grateful. I slowly open the door and peer inside. The room stinks of human, unwashed sheets, and uncirculated air. I wrinkle my nose but continue in. I can see the lump of Mom under the covers through the darkness, her back turned toward me. She rolls over as I near the side of the bed, and I realize this is the first time I've actually seen her face in days. I suck in my breath at what I see. Her skin is stretched across her cheekbones, her eyes hollow and dark in her sunken face. She's skin and bones, and her eyes look lifeless yet tortured. I bend down and give her an awkward hug, which she does not return.

"Bye, Mom. I hope you feel better," I mumble, not knowing what else to say.

She doesn't respond, just squeezes her eyes shut. A tear slips down, across the bridge of her nose.

I swallow back my own tears—I am *not* going *there* again. Stepping backward away from the bed, I run right into Gwen. I whip around and see her wide, frightened eyes, before I flee from the room as if the hounds of hell are chasing at my heels.

Before I know it, I'm in the kitchen again, catching my breath and trying to overcome the panic that has seized me. Dad walks into the kitchen, takes one look at my terrified face, and comes over to give me a hug, then takes hold of my shoulders and steps back so he can look intently into my eyes.

"It'll be okay, Kate. You'll get through this. *We'll* get through this, together, one day at a time. Right now, we need to leave for school. So, chin up and grab your stuff. Okay?" He cuffs me on the chin and studies me for a moment, as if to make sure I'm not going to crumple before his eyes, and turns away to grab the keys and head outside.

I don't say a word, just take a deep breath in through my nose, and exhale through my mouth, like the school guidance counselor taught us in fourth grade. I do it again, and a third time. Feeling slightly better, I grab my backpack and march out to the car without saying a word. I get into the front seat, buckle up, and sit perfectly still, looking straight ahead. I hear the others get into the car, but continue to stare through the windshield. It's as though I might crack if I move a single muscle.

When we arrive at my school, I climb stiffly from the car, walk through the doors and to my locker without seeing anyone or anything I pass. I vaguely hear someone calling my name, but it doesn't really register. I just keep walking, until I finally make it to my locker, and mechanically go about the business of emptying my backpack and pulling out the materials I'll need for first period. My mind is blank, and I imagine myself as a robot, going through the motions without feeling anything at all.

Suddenly, someone grabs hold of my arm, but I don't look at who it is. I hear my name from far off. The hand on my arm tightens and gives me a shake, turning me around so that I'm forced to look at its source.

Evelyn, of course, surrounded by fellow concerned friends and classmates.

"Kate! Kate, are you okay?" She asks anxiously, peering into my eyes.

I give a curt nod of my head, shake my arm loose, and head to my classroom. The bell rings just as I sit down at my desk, and it's the best sound I've heard in my entire life. Class starts and our teacher demands the students' attention—a guaranteed reprieve from prying eyes and questions.

I've managed to collect myself a bit by the end of class, and am prepared when Evelyn catches up with me on my way out of the room. Once again, she grabs my arm and gives it a shake.

"Kate! What is going on?" she asks, desperately.

"Nothing. I'm fine," I lie, looking somewhere past her eyes. I know she'll never buy it if I look straight at her.

It doesn't work, regardless. "No, you're not. Something's wrong, and you need to tell me what it is."

I lie again, "I'm fine. Really. I just need to get to class." I start walking, and Evelyn follows along, running into classmates in her effort to stay alongside me.

"Kate! You've got to talk to me! *What. Is. Wrong*?! Is it something with the beads?" Realization hits. "Is it your mom?" I don't react, but Evelyn draws in a deep breath, "It's your mom. Oh, no. What happened, Kate?" She asks, pleadingly.

I know she just wants to help, but I can't deal with telling her. Not here. Not right now. So I lash out.

"Look, Evelyn, I'm fine! I told you I'm fine, and I really am *fine*. I just don't want to talk to you right now, so leave me alone," I say, in a hard, angry voice. "You got that? Just leave me alone!"

I stalk away, leaving Evelyn behind me, her mouth hanging wide open, a wounded look in her eyes. I know that I've hurt her, and that none of this is her fault, but I press down the twinge of guilt, wrap myself back up in my robot persona, and head for my next class.

Lunch comes around, and everyone in the class is avoiding me, so I sit by myself and stare at the corn dog on my tray. I pick up my spork and swish the pears around on my plate, try a bite, then go back to swishing. I settle on my chocolate milk as the only nourishment I really need, not to mention the only thing I think I can keep in my stomach. Once the milk's gone, I proceed to stare at my tray until the lunch lady announces that it's time to return to class.

Unfortunately, I'm intercepted on my way, and this time it's not so easily avoided. The guidance counselor is approaching me, concern mixed with pity in her eyes.

"Katelyn? Can you come talk to me in my office, please?"

"I have class, Mrs. Tuttle."

"I understand that, dear. I've already told Mr. Forester that you'll be a little late to class."

I cast a longing glance down the hall toward my classroom and obediently turn into the office after Mrs. Tuttle.

"Have a seat, dear." Mrs. Tuttle motions to the chairs sitting near her desk. "Katelyn, your cousin, Evelyn, came to see me. She is very worried about you and says that you're not acting normal. I called your father, dear, and he told me what's going on."

I close my eyes for several seconds, then open them to look directly into the caring eyes of Mrs. Tuttle, who's perched on the edge of her desk. I say nothing, just continue to look at her, locked in my robot mind, silently daring her to call me "dear" one more time.

"Would you like to talk about it, Katelyn, dear?" she asks, kindly. Had it not been for that "dear," her compassion might have been enough to break through my veneer.

I shake my head. "No, thank you," I say, simply. I pull my gaze from her and look instead at the crucifix hanging on the wall.

"Your father and I thought it would be a good idea for you to leave school early and take the rest of the day off. I checked with your teachers, and you won't be missing too much. Unfortunately, your dad is still with your mom, helping her get settled, so he's not able to come pick you up. He suggested I call your Aunt Mary Ellen." She pauses, as if to gauge my reaction. I slide my gaze away from the crucifix for a moment, wanting to reassure her that I'm not cracking up like my mom. But I don't really feel that I can pull it off, so I look at the crucifix again.

Random thoughts begin to enter my mind. *Man, he was really skinny. What do those letters above his head mean again? I wonder if that crown of thorns still hurt after wearing it for so many hours, or if he'd gotten used to it?* I wish that I could reach up and pull it off the wall, to run my hands along the body on the cross, and maybe, just maybe, throw it at the window to see if either one will break.

Next thing I know, Aunt Mary Ellen is kneeling beside me. She places an arm around my shoulders and pulls my head toward hers in an effort to give me comfort. I resist and instead look at her. Her eyes are red rimmed and damp. She's obviously been crying. Great. This is just what I need. Another basket case to help the basket case. Good going, Mrs. Tuttle, Dad.

Aunt Mary Ellen takes my arm and pulls me up out of the chair. I rise without resistance. She pulls me into an embrace, but I don't hug her back. I hear her thank Mrs. Tuttle and tell her that she'll take care of me as she puts an arm around my shoulders and gently ushers me from the room. She stops briefly at the secretary's desk to sign me out, and then we walk down the hall and out of the school.

The sun is bright and I have to squint to adjust my eyes. I realize that I've forgotten my backpack but Aunt Mary Ellen says that Dylan or Evelyn will get it for me. She walks me to her car, opens the passenger door, and carefully tucks me into the seat, even reaching across me to fasten my seatbelt.

I don't pay any attention to where we're going, but realize at some point that we're not headed to my house, or Aunt Mary Ellen's, for that matter. I wonder dazedly what she's done with Maria, who hasn't started kindergarten yet, and is usually home with her mother. Before I know it, we come to a stop and Aunt Mary Ellen parallel parks the car on a relatively quiet street. She gets out of the car, and comes to my side to open the car door for me. I rise without her aid, and look around curiously, realizing through a fog that we've come to St. Joan of Arc, the same church where we attended Mass on Sunday.

Only five days ago, we were here, yet it seems like an eternity. I feel like an old woman, like I've aged in the short, yet vast time since we were last at this church.

Spotting a figure robed in black at the top of the church steps, Aunt Mary Ellen waves. She turns to give me a searching look as she says, "I hope you don't mind. I asked Joseph to join us."

The news doesn't pierce my robot persona, but I can see that she's waiting for a response, so I nod my head.

Aunt Mary Ellen continues awkwardly, "I didn't know the best place for us to go, but this seemed like it might be good. I know I always feel . . ." she pauses, as if searching for what to say, "closer to God. So . . . here we are." We climb the stairs without speaking. Uncle Joseph hugs me wordlessly before opening the heavy door for us. Mary Ellen chooses a pew close to the altar and sits, waiting for us to join her. I genuflect out of habit, and slide in, leaving enough room for Uncle Joseph on my right. I sit on the edge of the pew, feeling trapped, not at all sure that I want to be here. *Do I want to be closer to a God who allows things like this to happen?*

Still without speaking, Uncle Joseph lowers the kneeler bar, and Mary Ellen follows suit. He begins, "Lord, we pray today for Teresa, Kate's mom and our sister. Lord, please give her healing. We pray as well for Kate, and Paul and Gwen, and their father, Mike. Please comfort them through this difficult time, Lord. Blessed Mother, please be a mother to them, while Teresa cannot." Reaching into his pocket, he pulls out two rosaries, handing me one before making the Sign of the Cross and beginning the prayer. I hear the clacking of beads as Mary Ellen pulls her own rosary from her purse.

At first, I resist. I remain in my seat, trying not to hear the words or think of the stories. I vaguely hear him state, "The Agony in the Garden." My resolve weakens, and I begin to let the rhythm of the words wash over me.

"Hail Mary, full of grace, the Lord is with thee . . ."

I find my fingers moving along the beads in time with the prayer, though I know I'm not on the right one. The feel of the cool beads between my fingers is soothing. I gather the crucifix into the palm of my hand and run my thumb over it, grateful that I'm now able to touch what I had longed to touch in the counselor's office, but with no desire now to throw it toward a window.

As Uncle Joseph continues, "The Scourging at the Pillar," I lower myself from my seat, and kneel between my aunt and uncle. My reverie continues. My eyes are closed, and I fall into calm, until suddenly I see a slash of red across the insides of my eyelids. I startle, and then I see it again. I open my eyes, and everything around me is just as it should be, but when I close them again, I see another slash of red, and then another. I begin to recognize the scene, and understand that I am witnessing the mystery in my mind. The slashes of red are the whips, tearing into Christ's flesh. I hear a scream of agony, but I don't know whether it's coming from the man on his knees before me, or from an onlooker in the crowd. I reach out my hand to stop the torture, only to find that my flesh is torn by the whip as well. I snatch it back, nursing it against my stomach, as I continue to stand there, watching, unwilling or unable to help; I don't know which one.

Suddenly, I can't stand amidst the scene anymore. I open my eyes, and gasp for breath, falling back against the pew behind me. I look desperately around the church, needing the reassurance that it was all just in my head. Uncle Joseph abruptly halts his prayer and turns to me with concern written all over his face. The robot is gone, the bliss of nothingness removed, and I begin to sob in pure agony. Mary Ellen gathers me into her arms, rocking me gently back and forth, much as Dad did last night.

I cry in a way I never have before: deep, wrenching sobs that come from somewhere in the pit of my stomach and well up and out of me. I cry for Mom, for what she must be going through. I cry for myself and the pain I've experienced, losing her slowly over the past year. I cry for having to say goodbye to her empty eyes before we left the house, and for Gwen and Paul and Dad, who must go through this in their own ways as well. I cry for the things I said to Evelyn this morning, knowing that I hurt her when she was only trying to help. And I cry for a grandmother who's been lost to me for over a year now, for the loss of her generous smile, her warm hugs, the stories of her past, her hope for the future, and her rock-solid faith.

I thought I was all cried out after last night, but I was wrong. Clearly, seeing Mom this morning has pushed me to the edge. The vision of Jesus, being scourged, toppled me right over that precipice, and I begin to wonder . . . *why? Why would that have such an effect on me?*

Aunt Mary Ellen continues to rock back and forth, making shushing sounds as my sobs begin to abate. Finally, in need of an answer, I lift my head from her shoulder, which is now wet with my tears. I look at my aunt, and I understand that there's a reason why Dad wasn't available to pick me up from school early today. I need Aunt Mary Ellen right now; I need her experience as a mother, and her closeness to the woman that Mom used to be. Moreover, I need her *faith*, her *understanding*, and her *hope*.

She looks down at me with misty eyes filled with love, and I find myself telling her about what I saw.

"Aunt Mary Ellen, I *saw him*."

She looks at me, bewildered, but then her face clears and she smiles a knowing smile.

"You did, did you?" She asks, not questioning whether I really saw him. She seems to know, intuitively, that I did. She seems pleased, peaceful, even joyful to have heard my words. She looks toward Uncle Joseph, whose presence I had forgotten, then back at me, as she asks, "Would you like to tell us about it?"

"I . . . I was *there*," I say, in awe, "at the scourging. I saw them whipping him. It was . . . awful," I whisper, "just awful. I tried to stop them, but the whip hit *my* hand, and I—I was afraid." I look at the back of my hand now, where the whip would have lashed across it, but there is no sign of injury, and I suddenly feel very silly. It must have all been just in my head. I must be losing it too; maybe it runs in the family.

Uncle Joseph places a warm hand on my shoulder and I turn to look at him. His gaze is filled with warmth and reassurance as he intuitively responds to my concerns.

"Kate, you've received a special gift from God. Cherish it. Don't question whether it was real. It was. He gives us these experiences, sometimes. Not everyone is blessed with such a gift, and those who are may only receive one in their entire lives. But know this, Kate. God blessed you with this because he knows just what you need, and this—for the moment—is it."

"But what does it mean? Why didn't I stop them?"

"Kate, no one could have stopped Christ's death. It was part of God's plan for salvation. It *had* to happen, and God chose for it to happen in exactly the way that it did. He doesn't want you to *stop* it. He wants you to know that his Son died for *you*—because he loves you."

I nod my head, obediently, and try to think through everything he's said. I get it—sort of—but it still seems a little foggy, really.

Feeling Mary Ellen's hand on mine, I turn to her. She looks intently into my face and gives my hand a gentle squeeze. "Kate, I know that you're suffering right now. Jesus suffered too, so *he knows what you're going through*." She stops suddenly, and draws in a quick breath. Her eyes widen, and she smiles, a smile of wonder and awe.

"Kate. I think, maybe—" she glances around the nave of the church, as if searching for an answer there before settling her gaze on the statue of Mary, "Maybe you were standing in *her* place, in Mary's place. She watched her son suffer, the person that she loved most in the world. She watched him suffer, just as you are watching your mom suffer. Kate, perhaps it was Mary who gave you that insight." She grabs my arms, and gives me a gentle, excited shake. "Mary, the Blessed Mother. She wants you to know that she *understands* what you're going through, perhaps in a way that *no one else* can. She wants to be a mother to you, right now, when you need one most."

Aunt Mary Ellen grabs me up into a hug and actually begins to laugh. It seems the most ridiculous thing in the world that she's laughing at this most horrible point in our lives, but I begin to laugh too! Still laughing, she stands up, pulling me up with her, and gives me a gentle push to indicate that I should leave the pew. Then, she grabs my hand and pulls me toward the statue of Mary, where she falls to her knees and tugs me down beside her.

Still with an edge of laughter to her voice, she looks up at the statue and says, "Blessed Mother, we love you. We know that you are our mother too, and that we are *never* motherless. Thank you, Heavenly Mother. Thank you for the comfort that you have given to Kate. Please, continue to be with her through this difficult time. Be a mother to her when her earthly mother can't. Give her your wisdom, strength, and guidance. And be a mother for Teresa too. Help her to return to herself—to the person she *used* to be, the one our Lord made her to be." She reaches out her left hand and touches the feet of the statue, bowing her head. "Thank you, for being a mother to us all."

Still smiling, Aunt Mary Ellen turns to me and squeezes the hand that she still holds. "Would you like to say anything?"

I shake my head, mutely, not knowing what to say, before I turn my gaze up to the statue and reach my free right hand up to rest on her feet. I close my eyes and feel her comfort, almost as if she has placed a protective arm around my shoulders. I revel in that moment, saying nothing, thinking nothing—just enjoying the presence of this mother I didn't even know I had.

Finally, I open my eyes and look at Aunt Mary Ellen. She's clearly been watching me, enjoying being a witness to this moment, the moment I've come to recognize the Virgin Mary as *my* mother.

Aunt Mary Ellen smiles, letting go of the hand that I'd forgotten she held, and takes up her rosary beads. She turns to Uncle Joseph, who's now sitting in the pew, "All right," she says, brightly, "where were we?" He joins us where we kneel before the statue, and resumes the Rosary prayer where he had left off.

I blink, unable to transition so quickly, my mind still reeling from this new revelation. After a few Hail Marys, however, I'm able to focus, but it's different now. My focus on the mysteries is more complete, and I consider each one from the Blessed Mother's point of view, comparing her suffering to my own, and knowing that she can *definitely* relate to what I'm going through.

When we're done, I'm shocked by how very calm I feel. But this time I'm not numb like I was when I felt like a robot going mechanically through my day. I'm very aware of my surroundings, and able to think about what's going on with

Mom, but I don't feel totally freaked out over it anymore. Somehow, I know we'll get through it.

I think back over the past week, and realize that this is the fourth Rosary I've prayed in eight days, which is very likely more Rosaries than I've prayed in my entire life up to this point. When I think about it, I also realize that every time I've prayed the Rosary, whether with Evelyn or Aunt Mary Ellen, I've felt better afterward.

Every time, I've felt *hope*.

I savor that feeling, wanting to remember it, and how I found it in this Rosary prayer that I've always thought was . . . well, stupid. I feel guilty saying it now, but the truth is, I thought it was useless to spend twenty minutes praying, saying the same words over and over again, as if they were going to bring about some great spiritual revelation, or that some special request might be granted.

Now I know how wrong I was. This prayer is powerful. It does bring about spiritual revelation, like the one I had today: Mary is my mother in heaven. As for the favors, well. . . . That first time, Roger Billings *did* call almost immediately after we prayed for news of another bead. And every time I've prayed, I've felt better afterwards. So, maybe when I'm praying I'm growing closer to God, and that gives me calm and peace as a result?

The thoughts crowd my brain, and I really don't know what to make of it all. It's a relief when Aunt Mary Ellen stands, indicating that she's ready to go whenever Uncle Joseph and I are. I follow her lead, and Uncle Joseph does as well, a moment later.

"Where to now?" she asks, once we're out in the narthex of the church.

"Well, I didn't eat much for lunch . . ." I look up at her hopefully.

"Sure, we can grab a bite to eat."

She looks questioningly at Uncle Joseph, who quips, "I'm in! How about the Food Emporium?"

I was hoping for a burger, but I nod my head anyway, not wanting to seem rude. We leave the church in a warm silence, each presumably lost in our own thoughts.

Chapter Thirteen

Over our late lunch, I decide to ask Uncle Joseph the question that plagued me last night.

"Uncle Joseph, I don't get it. Evelyn and I prayed the Rosary last Friday, asking that we find another bead. Within a minute, the phone rang, and it was that old guy, Roger Billings, and he had found three beads, right? Then, on Sunday, Aunt Mary Ellen and I prayed the Rosary for Mom, but she was actually worse the next day—and *now* look what's happened. Evelyn and I prayed again the other night, to find more beads, and a lady called, but she really wasn't any help at all. She just said that she gave it to her drug-addicted brother and hasn't talked to him since.

"So, what I don't get is, why would God answer that first prayer, but not the others? If the Rosary really *works*, and if prayer *really works*, why isn't it working *now*?"

Uncle Joseph folds his hands on the table in front of him. He takes so long to answer, I begin to figure that there *is* no good answer, and that I'm just going to be disappointed.

"Well, Kate, we can only see a tiny slice of our lives, but God sees it all. He knows everything. So what you pray for—things you might want or think you need—sometimes they aren't in sync with God's will for your life. Very often he has something better for you." My expression turns doubtful.

Somehow, my mom going to the psych ward doesn't feel like "something better."

"I know it's hard to understand. We know that God loves us. He doesn't *want* bad things to happen to us, but he allows them because he has given us all free will. Because God is all good, and because he loves us, he will always bring good things out of what's bad. Our job, then, so to speak, is to trust God, recognize the good, and to look for ways that we can cooperate with God's plan for us."

Aunt Mary Ellen chimes in, "You know, I can already see some good things coming from all of this. You've made this connection with the Blessed Mother now, and that wouldn't have happened if you hadn't been so upset over what was going on."

I nod my head slowly, and Aunt Mary Ellen continues, "Maybe your mom just needed to get to a point where she actually had to seek help, you know?" She looks at Uncle Joseph and he nods his head in agreement. "Maybe her getting help and checking into a hospital is the best way for her to get well again. Maybe," now she's on a roll, "it's good for us—me, you, and Joseph—to have this time together, which we wouldn't be doing if everything was okay, right?"

I nod again, but I know that I'm not hiding my doubt very well. Aunt Mary Ellen sits back in her chair and gives a short laugh. "You know, we were all given a cross on the day that Mom died. Sometimes, I hate that cross, and wish we didn't have to bear it. But, when I think about that cross, I thank God for the grace he has given me to get through it, and I can see how it has made me stronger, and helped me to grow closer to Jesus, and to Mary." She pauses, and looks at me searchingly. "Am I making any sense?"

I shake my head and she laughs, "Well, thanks for your honesty," she says, and looks at Uncle Joseph. He takes the lead, but his words are really no help.

"Take some time to think about it, Kate, and pray about it too. God can bring a blessing out of every difficulty. God is the *only* one who can do that. Look for the blessings you can find, even in this situation."

I have other questions I'd like to ask, but my mind's reeling from all they've said, so I decide to wait until another time.

Aunt Mary Ellen must sense that I've had all I can handle. She changes the subject and starts asking me about school and the next play I'll audition for, and asks Uncle Joseph about the incoming students at the local college seminary, where he's the rector.

We finish up our meal and return to the car after saying our good-byes to Uncle Joseph. I'm amazed by how much better I feel now than I did this morning, and then I realize that there's something I need to do.

"Aunt Mary Ellen?" I ask.

"Yes," she responds as she maneuvers the car into traffic.

"Could you take me to Evelyn's house? I . . . I need to apologize to her. I was pretty awful this morning."

Aunt Mary Ellen glances away from the road to give me an understanding look. She pats my knee.

"Sure, hon, I can do that."

Five minutes later, we arrive at Evelyn's. I take a deep breath before opening the car door.

"I can walk home from here," I say.

Aunt Mary Ellen smiles and nods her head. It's as if she understands that I need the time alone. "I'll call your dad and let him know," she says.

I return her smile nervously, glad that she has thought of calling him. Oddly, it hadn't even crossed my mind that Dad might worry about me if I don't get home soon. Then I brace myself, walk to the back door, and give a tentative knock.

Evelyn answers the door, her expression unreadable. She steps back and motions me in. I walk into the kitchen, grateful to see that, for once, her mom isn't busy cooking there.

I pick at a spot in the granite countertop, not sure what to say. Finally, I manage to squeak out, "I'm sorry."

"It's okay. Your dad called my mom, so I know what's going on. But I'm not sure why you took it out on me," she says. I can hardly blame her for not letting me off the hook easily.

"I don't know," I say honestly. "I just didn't want to talk about it, definitely not at school. And I guess the easiest thing to do was to—to make you mad at me so you'd stop asking questions." I scuff my foot on the wood floor. "I'm sorry," I say again, stealing a glance away from my fingers and toward my cousin.

"I forgive you, Kate," she says, and gives me a much-needed hug. Then, she puts me out at arm's length and a smile lights her face. "And I've got news!"

Seeing the sparkle in her eyes, I know it must be news of a bead. "What! What is it?" I ask excitedly.

"Beth called while we were at school. I had a message when I got home. I didn't call her back because, well, I thought I should wait for you."

I squeal, grab her by the arms and we dance around in circles for a moment in excitement. Then, she grabs my hand and pulls me toward the phone in the kitchen.

"Here's her number," she says, handing me a sticky note. I stare at it dumbly until she says, "Come on, what are you waiting for?"

I grab the phone, press in the number, and wait for an answer. "Hi, Beth, it's Katelyn Roberts. You called and left a message earlier today?"

"Oh, yes. I'm sorry I didn't call back sooner. I heard from my brother—on Tuesday, the day after we spoke, actually. I went and saw him on Wednesday. I still can't believe it, but he finally did it. James went through rehab and just completed his recovery program last week. He looks amazing!"

Beth pauses and I realize that my mouth is hanging wide open. Evelyn, once again, has her head glued to mine so that she can hear what Beth is saying. She squeezes my hand and bounces up and down, but doesn't move her head, afraid to miss something.

"Katelyn, I told James that you were looking for the beads. And actually, he'd like to meet you. He seems to think that the bead I gave him played some role in his recovery."

"Really!" I squeak. Evelyn finally tears her head away from mine to look at me with huge eyes.

"Yes," she answers. "I understand if you're not comfortable, and I'd go with you and your parents, of course. James really is a great person, when he's sober."

I swallow, hard, at the mention of my "parents."

"Let me check with my dad, okay? I'd like to meet him, too. I think my cousin Evelyn will probably want to go, if that's okay?" My heart is racing, and my palms are a little sweaty. Beth assures me that Evelyn would be welcome, and I tell her that I'll call her back once we've asked our parents.

Evelyn runs right away and asks her mom, who's a little bit worried about us meeting a recently recovered drug addict. I suspect my dad will feel the same way, but Evelyn comes up with the perfect argument.

"Mom, we've gone and helped Beggars for the Poor hand out food to homeless people, and we've served the homeless at the St. Vincent de Paul Center. I thought you *wanted* us to see 'how other people live.'"

Ding ding ding! She hit the nail on the head. Aunt Susan gives Evelyn a long look, then says, "You're right, Evelyn. It is important for us to meet people with all kinds of different life experiences. I'll plan to go with you. I need to talk it over with your dad, but I think it should be fine."

Evelyn throws her arms around her mom's neck. "Thank you! Thank you! Thank you!" Then, she turns to me and says, "Okay, now for *your* dad."

"I think he'll say yes. He'll see it the same way your mom did," I assure her. I realize, though, that with everything that's happened today, calling right now to ask the question probably isn't the best idea.

"I'd better head home. I need to see how Mom's doing, and help fix dinner. I'll ask him later, and call you. Okay?"

"No need to worry about dinner, hon," Aunt Susan says. "I've got something in the oven to bring over for you guys. I can give you a ride home when it's done, okay? It should just be about thirty minutes or so."

What a relief! A night without worrying about dinner. I thank Aunt Susan, but tell her I'd actually like to walk home, if that's alright. I could still use that time alone.

With hugs to both Aunt Susan and Evelyn, I head for home in the bright afternoon sunshine. As I walk, I feel an unfamiliar bulk in my pocket and realize that I've still got Uncle Joseph's rosary. I suddenly start wondering if I should pray it again, even though I've already prayed once today. Remembering how calm I felt earlier, I decide to follow the inspiration, and make the Sign of the Cross.

This is the first time I've *ever* prayed a Rosary by myself, and I can't remember all of the mysteries. I fumble through, though, and when all else fails, summon memories of the image that I had earlier in the afternoon. This time it isn't so scary. I think about how Mary must have felt watching her son go through such terrible abuse, and how it feels for me to watch my Mom go through so much.

I finish when I'm a block away from my house. I don't remember the final prayers—the one that starts with "Hail, Holy Queen" or the last one where you say straight to God, "Oh my God" and then something or other. But I figure God, and Mary, and Jesus will be happy to have heard from me twice in one day, even if I didn't do it perfectly.

As I near the house, that wonderful calm settles on me again, and when I walk through the back door I say a little prayer that all will go well with my family.

Dad hears me open the door and comes to the kitchen to greet me. He folds me into a hug.

"Hey, sweetie. Sounds like you had a rough day."

"Yeah, but I'm okay now. Aunt Mary Ellen was really cool, and Uncle Joseph was there too."

"Good. I'm sorry I couldn't come get you but . . ." he leaves the sentence hanging, not wanting to say the words.

"I know, Dad. It's okay. Mom needed you. Aunt Mary Ellen and Uncle Joseph were really good substitutes." I assure him. "How's Mom doing?"

"She's good. Well, as good as can be expected. The facility is really nice, and the people were very kind. They'll take good care of her."

I manage a smile. "Good. That's good to hear."

Dad gives me another hug. "So, what'd you do with your aunt and uncle that left you feeling so much better?"

I feel a little awkward telling him, so I don't go into a whole lot of detail.

"Actually, we stopped at Saint Joan of Arc to pray, and then we went to the Food Emporium 'cause I really didn't eat my lunch and I was starving. We talked about . . . stuff," I finish awkwardly.

"Well, good. I'm glad you got a chance to talk. Mary Ellen and your mom always used to be so close, and I'm sure Joseph had some great insights and advice."

I nod my head. If he only knew, but I'm pretty sure he'd look at me as if I had grown another nose if I started telling him that Mary is my second mom. Some things just seem better left unsaid, I guess. Maybe I'll tell him more, someday.

"Um, Dad?" I query tentatively.

"Yes, hon?"

"Well, Evelyn got a call from a woman we talked to on Monday. She found one of the beads a while back. It had her brother's initials on it—J C L—so she gave it to him. He's—well, he *was*—homeless, and addicted to drugs. When we talked to her on Monday, she hadn't heard from him since she gave him the bead. But she called today to tell us that he contacted her Tuesday, and that he's gone through a recovery program and now he's sober." I continue on in a rush, "He—he wants to meet us. He thinks the bead had something to do with his getting clean, and well, you know how it's good for us to meet people with different backgrounds and life experiences, and all . . ."

"What?" Dad asks, looking rather blindsided.

"Well, I was hoping maybe we could go see him." I finish, then look up at him with my sweetest begging eyes.

"Well, you and Evelyn are most certainly not going by yourselves!"

"No, of course not! Aunt Susan has already said she'll go with us, and you can come too if you want to."

"Kate, with your mom being gone I'm overwhelmed. I hate to leave Gwen and Paul here alone, so it's not that easy.

And I think bringing them along would be a bit much. When were you thinking of going?"

"I don't know . . . I'd like to go soon, this weekend, maybe?"

"I guess it's okay for you to go, but I would really like to go with you."

I can see Dad's overprotective "man" side coming to the surface. Clearly, he doesn't feel that Aunt Susan is enough to protect us from a potentially unstable, formerly homeless drug addict. I suppose he's got a point.

Fortunately, I'd already thought about this. "What if Gwen could go to Aunt Susan and Uncle David's, and hang out with Ava, and Paul could go to Aunt Mary Ellen's, and play with Daniel?" I suggest, hopefully.

"That might work. We can ask Aunt Susan when she delivers dinner here shortly. Would you mind calling your Aunt Mary Ellen to ask about Paul? I've got some work I really need to catch up on since I wasn't in the office today."

"Yes! Yes, I will!" I take off, running for the phone, then realize I've forgotten something. I run back to Dad, throw my arms around his neck, and give him a huge hug. "Thank you so much, Daddy!"

He returns my hug in his warm, crushing, *dad* way. I relax into him before peeling away to complete our arrangements.

A half hour later, I've talked to both of my aunts, and Beth, and the plans are all set. Tomorrow afternoon, we will meet James—the potentially-unstable, formerly-homeless drug addict—at a coffee shop downtown. I can't wait!

Chapter Fourteen

I feel nervous as we sit at the coffee shop waiting for Beth
and her brother, James. What do you say to a person who, up
until a few months ago, was homeless and addicted to
drugs? Will he be weird? Or missing all of his teeth? Will his
skin be all pitted and peeling off, like the pictures I've seen
of meth heads? I fiddle with the tails of my red blouse as
they lie on my lap, and look anxiously around the coffee
shop.

I didn't even think to ask Beth what she looks like, or
what she would be wearing. For all I know, they're already
here. There are several tables that have a man and woman at
them, but they all seem pretty absorbed in each other, not
like they're waiting for someone. So I keep my eyes on the
door, expecting them to come through any minute.

Fifteen minutes later, they still haven't arrived. Evelyn,
Aunt Susan, and I play Hangman on a napkin. Dad is clearly
getting a little irritated. We had planned to wait to get our
drinks until they arrived, but Dad finally pushes his chair
back.

"Let's go ahead and get drinks. Maybe that will help the
wait. Kate, here's my cell phone. Why don't you try calling
Beth while I'm ordering?"

He gets everyone's drink orders and heads for the
counter. I fish Beth's number out of my pocket, grateful that
Dad reminded me to bring it.

Unfortunately, I realize when voicemail picks up, the only phone number I have for Beth is her work number, and of course she isn't there on a Saturday.

Just at that moment, though, a man and a woman walk through the door and look around the coffee shop. The woman is tall, slender, and pretty, with rich auburn hair cut in layers that frame her face. The man looks older than she is, which surprises me, since she mentioned that he was her younger brother. He's clean shaven, but his skin looks weathered and his hair is heavily peppered with gray.

The woman's gaze settles on us when she sees me watching them. She smiles tentatively, I smile back, and they approach our table, just as Dad arrives with the drinks.

We all stand to make the introductions, and then Aunt Susan heads to the counter to get coffees for Beth and her brother. James speaks up, in a deep and friendly baritone.

"I'm sorry we're so late. I've started working at the mission, and there was a situation that I needed to help with." I wonder what the "situation" might have been, but James clearly is not prepared to talk about it. Having just met the man, I'm certainly not going to ask.

He pulls back a chair for his sister, waits for her to sit, then takes a chair for himself, as the rest of us resume our seats. Aunt Susan returns with their coffees, sitting down just as James begins.

"So, I understand you've been looking for this." He sets the bead in the middle of the table.

I nod mutely. He seems friendly enough, but I find myself intimidated by him. I guess it's because I know about his past. The fact that he *is* missing several teeth doesn't help, either.

James picks the bead up again, staring at it as he holds it in his palm, as if it were a cherished possession, rather than just a small bead. "There's something special about this bead. But you know that already, don't you? That's why you're looking for it."

Again, I nod, but don't say anything.

"I think my sister told you a little bit about my story, but I'm sure she didn't go into details. I've always been a private person, and she respects that. But I feel that I should tell you the whole story—or at least more than I would typically tell someone I just met. So, here goes."

"Beth and I lost our parents when she was nineteen and I was sixteen. Mom died suddenly of a heart attack, and Dad died a few months later." James's mouth twists bitterly. "That left Beth responsible for me, which couldn't have been easy, since I was a pretty rebellious teenager, and I was trying to pretend I wasn't hurting. I had already fallen in with the wrong crowd, and when my friends started doing drugs, the easy thing to do was to follow right along. I wanted to escape from life, you know, from losing my mom and dad, and being dependent on my big sister."

Beth smiles a bit sadly.

"We started smoking a little marijuana on the weekends. It didn't seem like that big a deal. Then one day a friend got a hold of some methamphetamine. We all agreed we'd try it—just once—and then we'd never do it again.

"It wasn't that easy, though. One time wasn't enough. I wanted more, and I was willing to do anything to get it. I stole from Beth . . . took everything I could find. All to get my next hit. Finally, she had to kick me out."

He looks at Beth, whose face is filled with guilt. She starts, "I still feel so terrible about that, but I just didn't know what else to do—"

"No, Beth, you did what you had to. I would have taken everything you had, eventually." He turns back to me and

Evelyn, "I was out of my mind. I didn't care about anyone or anything, except how I was going to score my next hit."

"I wound up living in a homeless community down by the canal. Everybody had their little spot. I managed to find some old shipping pallets, and I made a tiny shack out of that. It was a dangerous place, and you had to watch your back constantly, 'cause most of the people were like me—willing to do anything to get their drug of choice.

"I was angry that Beth kicked me out, so I didn't contact her for a long time. After a while, though, I thought maybe she'd give me money, or at least some food. So I finally called her, and after that I'd call her every couple of months or so. She'd meet me at what became our regular spot. I knew I was breaking her heart, but I just couldn't stop what I was doing. She'd bring me food, and maybe clothes, socks, shoes, things like that. But not money. Never money. She knew what I'd do with it." James runs a hand across his face, which is creased and worn like that of an old man.

"Of all my friends who started doing drugs with me, only one other has gotten clean. Three of them are dead, over-dosed or killed by some stupid thing they did because of the meth. Two are in jail, one of them for murder, the other for armed robbery." He sits, looking at his coffee, for a long moment.

"Yeah, I'm lucky to be alive. Or blessed, I guess I should say." He looks up now, looking each of us in the eye and then looking at his sister. "I made my apologies to Beth earlier this week. What I did to her was terrible, inexcusable, and I wouldn't blame her if she refused to forgive me." His bottom lip quivers a bit, and Beth takes his hand in hers, giving it a squeeze for reassurance.

"I owe my recovery to her not giving up on me, and to this bead." He holds the bead up, between his thumb and finger. "Beth tells me it's from a rosary, and I guess I'm not surprised. We grew up Catholic, but when Mom and Dad died, I stopped going to Mass, stopped praying, and stopped believing. I just didn't get how God could let such a bad thing happen. Beth kept going to church, and I suppose her faith is the reason she's been so generous and loving all these years, and so . . . incredibly forgiving." James looks at Beth again, and then settles his gaze on me.

"Last fall, I felt this overwhelming urge to call my sister. I happened to have a quarter in my pocket, so I walked to a pay phone and dialed her number. We arranged to meet and when we did, she gave me this bead. This silly little bead, on a cheap chain. I took it, just to make her happy. But honestly? I was thinking about how much I might be able to get if I pawned it or traded it. I'm ashamed to admit that I was trying to think of a dealer whose initials were the same as mine: J C L. Fortunately, I didn't figure that out, and I still had the bead around my neck the following day when I came down from the hit I took right after I met with Beth." He shakes his head, as if still struggling to believe the story he's about to tell.

"I was in my little pallet home, huddled against the cold morning air, shivering the way I always would when coming down from a hit. All of a sudden, my little hut got very warm, and my shivering stopped. A woman stood in front of me."

Chills run down my spine. Evelyn grabs my arm and we look quickly at each other as James continues, "She was *beautiful*—absolutely *beautiful*—but it wasn't really anything about her face, or her hair, or anything like that; it was her *joy*. She had so much joy in her that you could see it on her face, and she actually *lit up* my little shack."

James sets the bead down and leans forward in his chair, gripping the edge of the table. "She didn't say anything, but I knew who she was. *Mary*. I don't know how I knew, I just *knew*."

James pauses, and I nod mutely as I look around the table. Beth is misty eyed, and Aunt Susan bears an awe-filled expression, while Dad seems politely doubtful. Evelyn's eyes are wide with shock and excitement. I return my focus to James as he goes on, "I also knew why she was there—to help me straighten up my act. Thoughts filled my head about the terrible things I'd done, and the people I'd hurt, but also about the person I could become: a trustworthy brother, a loyal friend, maybe even a husband, a father . . ." he smiles, looking around the table. "Right then and there, I decided I would go get help. The woman smiled, even more radiant than before, and held out her arms to me." James' face lights up. He closes his eyes, seeming to savor the memory, before he opens them and says, matter-of-factly, "Then she disappeared."

He sits back in his chair now, a look of wonder returning to his face. "I could have sworn the chain with the bead was still around my neck. I never took it off. But somehow, I found that I was holding the bead in my hand. I *know* I didn't put it there." He shakes his head, as if he's still having a hard time believing it all, as the rest of us sit in rapt attention.

"It took me a while to recover my wits, but when I did, I put the chain back around my neck, packed up my few belongings, and walked to the mission." He looks at Beth as if making a promise, "I've been clean ever since, and I'll never go back to what I was before."

Now James leans forward again, and looks at Evelyn, then at me, "So, you see, I believe this bead is special. But, like I said, I think you already know that."

I can't think of anything I can say to such an amazing story. I look at Dad, sitting across the table from me, and I'm startled to see that he looks a little bit . . . sick. But then he speaks up and I'm shocked by what he says.

"Yes, James, you're right. So far, we know of three people besides Kate who have been given one of the beads, and something extraordinary happened to each of them shortly afterward. I didn't believe it—and I'm not sure I believe it now—but it does appear as though there is something special about them."

Evelyn kicks me under the table, hard, and I jump. Everyone looks at me so I feel like I have to say something. I add, "Yes, one girl was in a really bad car accident, but she wasn't hurt, and a little girl has been cured of cancer. And then there's you . . ." I pause. "And the way I found *my* bead, well . . . that was kind of special too, but I haven't seen any miracles yet."

Now, Aunt Susan speaks up, "Maybe there's another kind of miracle for you, Kate. Perhaps, finding the first bead, and discovering all these amazing stories . . . perhaps this is all working a miracle in your *heart.*"

I realize that she's right. This little bead, which I roll between my fingers now as it hangs around my neck— finding it, and searching for the others, hearing the miracles that have happened . . . this little bead has brought me a Mother I never knew I had, a calming prayer that I never cared about before, and faith in a God I can really trust and believe in.

I nod my head slowly, still rolling the bead between my fingers. "I think you're right, Aunt Susan." I look her in the eyes. "I think you're right."

Chapter Fifteen

We leave Beth and James with hugs and handshakes. Somehow, after our brief meeting, we seem to feel close to each other, despite the fact that we've just met. Each of us congratulates James on his recovery, and we promise to keep both him and Beth posted on any other beads we find.

James says that a man has just come into the mission who has the same initials, so he was thinking of giving the bead to him, in hopes of it leading to the man's recovery as well. We agree that it's a great idea, though I feel a pang of guilt at not retrieving Aunt Janey's bead.

I'm anxious to talk to Dad about what he said, about the beads being special, but I can't do it with Evelyn and Aunt Susan in the car. When we drop them off, we pick up Gwen and then head over to Aunt Mary Ellen's to get Paul.

When we arrive, Aunt Mary Ellen invites us to stay for dinner. Dad and I look at each other, smile, and accept her offer gratefully. Aunt Mary Ellen's no Aunt Susan in the cooking department, but today she's making chicken stir-fry, which sounds like a huge improvement over the reheated leftovers I was planning.

Dad excuses himself to go look for Uncle Bob, while Gwen follows the noise of the kids playing in the basement. I pull up a barstool in the kitchen and watch while my aunt prepares the meal. She asks me about our meeting and I fill her in. Her eyes sparkle, and when I finish telling her the story, she says, "Isn't God amazing? The way he works . . . Wow." She doesn't speak for a few minutes, seeming to ponder all that's happened, and I do the same.

Yes, I guess God is pretty amazing, isn't he?

Then I start to think about little Hannah, and Mom's bead. "Aunt Mary Ellen?"

"Yes?" She looks up from the strawberries she's cutting.

"Do you think if we had Mom's bead, that it would do something special for *her*?"

Aunt Mary Ellen looks down at the strawberries, but her hands remain still. She shakes her head, and looks back at me with sad eyes. "I don't know, honey. Maybe it would. But it isn't really the bead that's doing any of these things. You know that."

"You're right. But it just really stinks. We know where it is, but it's too far away to just go get it. Plus, because it means so much to Hannah, Dad says that we shouldn't ask for it back . . ." Suddenly, an idea dawns on me, and I say brightly, "What if I traded her? What if I gave her *my* bead, and she gave me mom's in exchange?"

Aunt Mary Ellen nods her head, "Well, yes . . . that might work, if you're sure you don't mind parting with yours. I know that it's very special to you. But you'll still need to find a way to make the exchange."

My shoulders slump. "Oh, yeah. You're right."

"Why don't you mail them, Kate? That would be very simple."

I shake my head adamantly. "No way. You remember a few years ago, when Mom sent Aunt Liz's Christmas present out to Denver, and she never got it?" Mary Ellen nods her head and I keep going, "I'm not taking any chance on these beads getting lost." I shake my head adamantly again.

"I understand that, Kate, I do. But I don't see you taking a trip down to Florida with everything else that's going on."

Another idea dawns, and I dare to ask: "*You* could take me."

I've clearly startled her, and she blusters a bit. "Kate, I've got five kids of my own to take care of. I can't just leave them and drive to Florida on a moment's notice."

She's right. It was thoughtless of me to ask, yet I can't help feeling a little put off and totally disappointed. I try to hide my feelings, and manage a weak smile, but I can't look her in the eye.

"I know. I'm sorry. I shouldn't have asked," I say.

Aunt Mary Ellen lays down the knife and walks around the island to where I sit on a barstool. She lays a hand on my knee. "There's no need to be sorry, Kate. I understand. I'd like to be able to go, but I just don't know how I could work it out." She gives me a hug and I squeeze my eyes to keep the tears from starting again. What is it about people being sympathetic that always makes me cry?

I belatedly realize that I'm sitting here, doing nothing, while Aunt Mary Ellen does all of the chopping, cooking, and cleanup, so I ask what I can do to help. She puts me on table-setting duty, and I'm happy to have something to busy my hands and give me an excuse to hide my face—and my emotions—from her all too perceptive eyes. I set the kitchen table for the little kids and the dining room for the adults and older kids.

Just as Aunt Mary Ellen is calling everyone to the table, the phone rings. She glances at the caller ID and decides to answer it. She talks for a few minutes, then comes into the dining room.

"That was Susan. She's having the whole family over for brunch after Mass tomorrow."

"Sweet!" I announce, then think to ask, "Dad, can we go?"

"I don't know, sweetheart. We've been gone all day today, and I have a lot of things I need to do around the house. I'll think about it, and let Aunt Susan know after we get home, okay?"

"Okay," I say, disappointed.

We say grace, and dinner proceeds comfortably. It occurs to me that my dad is sitting here, surrounded by my *mom's* family—not the one he grew up in—yet, he seems content. I realize what a blessing that is. I have friends at school who talk about their mom not getting along with their dad's family, or their dad not getting along with their mom's family. It seems like what we have might be pretty rare, and—especially now, when my mom isn't here and my dad's parents are far away in South Carolina—it's good to have this great big extended family. But, I suppose I can't really blame Dad if spending all day Saturday with his wife's family is enough, and he's ready to have some time to himself on Sunday.

Dinner is delicious. Afterward, I volunteer to clean up and draft Mary Ellen's two oldest kids, Thomas and Zach, to help me. We're nearly done when I go back into the dining room to wipe the table and overhear Aunt Mary Ellen talking with Dad in a low voice.

"Mike, I really hope you'll be able to make it to Mass and Susan's house tomorrow morning."

"Mary Ellen, I'd like to be able to, but I really do have a lot of catching up to do."

"I understand, Mike, and I can take the kids for you if you like. But I think they'd really like to have you with them as well. You're their rock right now—they need you more than ever."

I hear Dad draw a ragged breath, and I imagine him running his hands through his thick, brown hair. "I know you're right. But this is taking a lot out of me, too, and I really need some down time to get ready for whatever the week may hold."

"Well, think about it, Mike. Like I said, I understand. I'm happy to pick up the kids and take them to Mass, and then to Susan's, if you'd prefer."

"Let me see how I'm feeling after tonight, and I'll text you in the morning, okay? Can you go ahead and let Susan know that the kids, at least, will be at brunch?"

Feeling guilty for eavesdropping, and realizing that the conversation is over, I tiptoe out of the dining room and back into the kitchen. The boys are nowhere to be seen, despite the fact that there are still a few dishes to be washed and counters to be cleaned. I set to work, then step back proudly ten minutes later, surveying my accomplishment—a sparkling clean kitchen. Next, I head to the living room, where Dad and Uncle Bob are discussing the upcoming NFL draft. Quickly bored by their conversation, I go find Thomas and Zach playing video games, with Gwen watching, while Maria combs her baby doll's hair nearby. Paul is outside with Isaac and Daniel, playing basketball. Having no interest in video games, baby dolls, or basketball, I decide that it is *definitely* time for us to go home. Fortunately, Dad and Uncle Bob have hit a lull in the conversation when I return to the living room, and Dad agrees when I suggest that it's time for us to take off. We drag Paul away from his basketball game, while Gwen happily jumps to her feet, clearly bored by the boys' video game.

As we head home, it feels so weird that Mom isn't with us. I think about what she might be doing tonight. Do they have a TV? Is she reading a book? Or do they have some sort of social group arranged for Saturday nights? Do they offer Mass, or any sort of church service, where she is? And will she attend if they do? My guess is probably not.

Feeling guilty, I realize that, while it's weird that Mom isn't here, I don't miss the heavy layer of sadness that has surrounded our family whenever she's been around for the last year. I look out the window of the car, and try not to think about it.

⤝

Sunday dawns soaking wet, with a chill in the air. I've set my alarm clock and wake up at seven thirty. Dad's already up, sitting at his computer in the office.

"Hey," I say, leaning on the office doorway.

"Good morning, sweetheart." Dad turns in his chair and gives me a small smile. "Did you sleep okay?"

"Yeah. You?"

"I've had better nights." His smile doesn't quite reach his eyes.

"Can we go to Mass and Aunt Susan's?" I ask, hopefully.

"I really can't go, hon. But your Aunt Mary Ellen is going to take you. Okay?"

"Yeah. Okay, Dad." I try to hide my disappointment. I really wish he'd go. I had hoped, after he admitted that the beads seemed to be doing something special, that maybe . . .

"Dad?"

"Yes, hon?"

"Yesterday, when we met with Beth and James, you said that you thought maybe the beads *are* special."

Dad shifts in his chair and glances at his computer. "Yes, I did say that, didn't I?" I hear the regret in his voice.

"So, did you mean it?" I ask.

"Well, Kate, I suppose you're old enough to have this conversation. I'm a realist. I don't believe in things that I can't see. The whole notion of there being a "God" somewhere out there, well, I just can't understand how that's possible, you know? But I've always respected your mom's desire to raise you kids as Catholics, and I can see how believing in something can make things easier for people. I've just never been able to believe it myself. My parents aren't religious, but they taught me good values, self-confidence, and how to be a responsible person, so that's what I've always done."

He takes in a deep breath. "Your mom's family throws me for a loop, sometimes. Your grandmother, well . . . there was a—a peace about her. She went through some incredibly difficult times and maintained a strength and a peace that was nothing short of *remarkable*. And she always said that it was her faith that got her through. When your grandpa died she lost her best friend. Yet, there was a certain kind of . . . *joy*. Do you remember that?" He looks up at me, questioningly.

I nod as I recall, "Yeah. She told me once that his pain was over, and that he had been such a wonderful man, she knew he was headed for a better place."

Dad smiles, "Exactly. I can still remember the *hope* in her face." He leans back in his chair, thinking. "Then there's your Aunt Mary Ellen, and the way she lives her life. And your Uncle Joseph, the fact that he's given his life to serve as a priest, and he's so darn *happy*. I mean, he's given up *so much*—a wife, children, a career—and yet, he's one of the happiest people I know." Dad shrugs his shoulder and stares blankly at his computer screen.

"I've always dismissed all of this religious stuff, and figured that some people just need to believe in something bigger than us, or have someone else in charge. But then, you found that one, little bead. I don't want to call the stories you've heard *miracles*, but there's no denying that they're *amazing*. As a realist, I can't dismiss them as mere coincidence. It seems to go beyond that.

"So, sweetie, I'm ready to admit that there's something special going on. It's got me thinking about all the people of faith I've known—Grandma, Mary Ellen, Joseph. When I met your mom, and her family, I dismissed their kindness as the result of being from such a great family. Then I met Natalie, you remember, from the office?"

"Yes. She was really nice."

"Exactly. I figured she had to have a similar background—a great, loving family. But then I learned that her father was abusive and her mother abandoned her. And yet, look at how she turned out. She positively lights up our whole office."

He shrugs, "Anyways, it's all got me thinking that maybe, just maybe, there's something to this whole God thing. But I'm not ready to take any leaps of faith myself, at least not yet, and probably not for a long time."

I nod my head, trying to take it all in. I always knew that my dad wasn't a *believer*, but he's never explained his perspective to me before. I feel sad for him. Sure, I haven't always had the strongest faith, but I've always known that there was a God, someone who was *really big*, and who loved me. I think about the journey I've been on these past few weeks, and how, in such a short period of time, my faith has become so important to me, and how it has given me so much peace and calm in such a difficult time. I try to imagine what it would be like to go through all of this *without* my faith, and the bottom line is this: I'm really glad that I don't have to.

I look at my hands, which I've been twisting together in front of me, and then I peer at Dad. "So, you're sure you won't come to Mass with us today?" I ask in a small voice.

"Yes, hon. I'm sure. Like I said, I've got a lot to do. And going to Mass . . . well, that would be a stretch for me. In a number of ways."

I nod my head again, resolving to pray for my dad, and leave the room to grab breakfast before hopping in the shower to get ready for Mass.

Aunt Mary Ellen picks us up early, so that we can all pray a Rosary before Mass. Gwen and Paul aren't happy with this, but they manage to sit without squirming too much. The Mass carries a new beauty for me, as I think about what Dad said about Grandma, Aunt Mary Ellen, Uncle Joseph, and Natalie, and the strength of their faith. I think about the fact that millions of people across the world will celebrate the same Mass, hear the same readings, in probably hundreds of different languages, and all receive the Eucharist. I pay close attention, and think about little things that normally escape my notice, like how *right* it is that we don't sing alleluia during this season of Lent. I realize that my family is going through our saddest and most difficult time, when the Church is focusing on the most sad and difficult time in history—the death of Christ.

As we head to Aunt Susan's house, I ride in the front seat. Gwen is in the back, with little Maria. Paul is riding with Uncle Bob in their van, with the rest of Aunt Mary Ellen and Uncle Bob's kids. The rain continues to pour down, and the windshield wipers swish rapidly across the glass.

Nearly shouting to be heard over the pounding rain, Aunt Mary Ellen broaches a subject that I—somehow—hadn't even considered.

"Uncle Matthew and Aunt Janey, and Uncle Jonathan and Aunt Kathy will be there today. I think you ought to tell them about the beads yourself."

"Uhhh—" I stammer. I don't know why the idea of telling my uncles and aunts makes me so nervous—I usually love being the center of attention, and holding a big secret is a rare and unusual privilege. But the mere thought of sharing this particular secret has my palms sweating and my heart racing.

Gwen leans forward, "I'll tell everybody! I think it's cool!"

I glare at her. I definitely don't want *her* sharing *my* story.

I clear my throat, watching the windshield wipers swish back and forth.

"I'll do it." I say, but no one hears me over the din of the rain.

"Do you want to tell them?" Aunt Mary Ellen says loudly, oblivious to my prior response.

She glances at me, and I nod my head as I begin to think about what I'm going to say.

⟡

When we arrive, I look around the kitchen, crowded with family members, and feel a pang of sadness when I don't see my dad. I had held out hope that he'd come, even though he said he had too much to do. His presence would have made this a whole lot easier, I think.

After everyone has eaten, Aunt Susan sends the younger kids to the basement to watch a movie. The rest of us—the adults, Dylan, Evelyn, and I—gather in the great room, sitting on sofas, and chairs that have been carried in; or standing, leaning against the doorway, the mantle, and the desk. A few even sit on the floor. It's a cozy scene, all these people who care about each other and don't see nearly enough of each other anymore. The rain pounds on the window pane, but it's warm and comfortable inside.

Aunt Mary Ellen announces that I have something I'd like to share. All eyes turn toward me as I begin my story, starting from the beginning, when I found my bead in the field. I cover every detail but one—I avoid using James' name, or mentioning his initials. I don't want Aunt Janey to know that we could have retrieved her bead, but didn't. By the time I come to the end of it, there have been many questions, a few tears, and much excitement. Uncle Joseph smiles warmly at me, then turns to the rest of the family.

"I first heard Kate's story last weekend. Mary Ellen called me and asked me to impart my 'priestly wisdom,'" he states, with a smirk. "It is an amazing story, especially since this has happened within our own family. But I do want to caution everyone that it's important to keep our focus on God. It's easy to hear a beautiful story like this and start to think that there is some sort of 'magic' at work. That's dangerous, and it's also incorrect." He looks around the room, leaning forward in his seat to add, "What's working here is God's love and his grace.

"God gives us the seven Sacraments through the Church, and he also gives us sacramentals. Sacramentals are *things*—like rosary beads or religious medals or crucifixes," he gestures toward the crucifix hanging above the doorway. "They are signs or symbols of faith, and are meant to help us live our faith more fully. They can help bring us to God's grace, but they don't have any power of their own.

"The amazing events Katelyn has told us about seem to be associated with the beads, but they are not actually coming from the *beads themselves*. They are answers to the prayers that have been prayed on each of these beads, for many, many years, by a woman of deep faith, who trusted

God. Mom," he adds gently. "And maybe they're also the result of our Blessed Mother Mary praying with us and for us. These stories show us how much God loves us, how much he listens to and answers our prayers. Prayer is powerful. Mom knew the power of praying the Rosary in her own life, and more than a few of us have experienced it as well. I think all of this is reminding us that we're all connected, and that even one single prayer—one Our Father, or one Hail Mary—counts. That's the power of a single bead."

Chapter Sixteen

"Uncle Joseph?" I ask.

"Yes, Kate?"

"Mom's bead . . . it's down in Florida with Hannah, the little girl who used to have cancer. Do you—do you think that we should go get it?"

"Well, again, the bead, in and of itself, doesn't possess any special power. That said, there are many stories of miraculous events surrounding sacramentals. Have you heard of Blessed Mother Teresa of Kolkata?"

"Yes," I answer. "I did a report on her last year. She served the poor in India, and founded the Missionaries of Charity, right?"

"That's right." He turns, sharing the story with everyone in the room. "I heard recently about a man who met Mother Teresa on a plane, and she gave him her rosary. The experience of meeting her brought him back to the faith. He gave the rosary to a friend who was sick, and, after that person experienced a miraculous healing, they lent the rosary to other friends and family who they thought might benefit from it. Word spread, and he began to receive requests from all over the United States. They mailed the rosary all over the country, and the people who prayed with it did, indeed experience healing, comfort, and peace."

I nod my head, remembering that, a few years after Mother Teresa died, a woman in India had a huge tumor, but then woke up one morning and the tumor was gone. The Missionaries of Charity had been praying for Mother Teresa's intercession. The Pope recognized it as a miracle, and Mother Teresa was beatified—the first step in being named a saint—a few years later.

I focus my attention back on Uncle Joseph as he continues, "So, while a rosary bead, in and of itself, doesn't possess power, God can make use of an object—or a situation, or a person, or *anything*, for that matter—to give us his grace."

He directs his gaze toward me, "To answer your question: Yes, Kate, I do think that there would be value in having that bead. I think that having it in her possession might help your mom remember that God is still there for her, and that he always has been."

I suck in my breath. These words, coming from the priest in the family, give me hope. Surely *someone* will agree to go to Florida?

Dylan, of all people, speaks up. "I'll take her down to Florida."

Aunt Susan's face twists into a look of horror. "No, you will not, young man."

"What? I'm eighteen years old! There's no reason I can't do it. We can go over spring break. I'll maintain the speed limit . . . the *whole* way."

"I'm sorry, Dylan, but I'm just not comfortable with it. I've heard too many stories of kids driving to Florida for spring break, and . . ." She shakes her head. "I'm just not okay with it. It's not safe." She takes a deep breath. "I'll do it."

I run to Aunt Susan, who's sitting perched on the arm of the sofa, and throw my arms around her neck.

"Really? Thank you, Aunt Susan!"

"Kate, this is *not* going to be a fun trip. It's a long drive down there, and we won't be stopping to see the sights. Dylan can come with us, to take turns with the driving and give me a break. Evelyn can come too, for that matter, and both of you can drive part of the way as well. That way no one has to drive for too long, and you girls can get more experience before you get your licenses. We'll do it over the weekend, so David will be here with Ava." She turns to Uncle David, "If that's okay with you, of course?" she adds as an afterthought.

Uncle David's usually pretty easygoing, and this time is no exception. He nods his head and smiles at Aunt Susan, "Yes, darling. That's fine."

Aunt Susan looks at me, "Of course, your dad has to approve it as well, Kate."

⁕

Dad's not quite so easy to sell on the idea, but after much begging and cajoling, he eventually agrees to let me go. He insists that we take Mom's SUV, which he claims is safer than Aunt Susan's minivan.

Dad calls Mr. Billings to get the phone number, then places the call to Florida, putting it on speaker. Hannah's mom answers.

"Hello, Mrs. Layton. This is Mike Roberts, and I've got my daughter Kate with me as well."

There's a polite but curious murmur on the other end.

"I understand that your daughter, Hannah, has three special beads, which your father gave to her?"

"Oh, yes! Are you the family that they came from? I've been wanting to thank you for letting us keep them. They truly seem to have worked a miracle for Hannah."

"Yes, Mrs. Layton. The beads came from my mother-in-law's rosary. We were very pleased to hear about Hannah's recovery, and happy for any part that the beads may have played in that." Dad looks at me, considering his next words carefully.

"Mrs. Layton, one of the beads that Hannah has bears the initials of my wife, Teresa. Teresa has been . . . ill, lately, and we were hoping that, perhaps . . ."

"Oh, you'd like her bead back? Of course! It's yours—hers—we could never keep it if she needs it. I'd be happy to mail it back—"

"No!" I speak up. "No, I'm afraid that it might get lost in the mail. My aunt has offered to drive me down there to get it. We talked about coming next weekend."

"Oh, sure, I think we can make that work. When do you think you'll get here? Will you need a place to stay?"

"Um, I'm not sure what time we'll get there. But, yes, a place to stay would be . . . wonderful, if it's not too much trouble?"

"No trouble at all! We'd be honored to have you. Like I said, those beads led to a miracle for Hannah, and we'd like to do whatever we can to help you."

"Mrs. Layton?" I ask.

"Yes?"

"Will Hannah miss the bead? Does she need to have three? 'Cause if she does, I have a bead, with my initials, and I'll give it to her. I just really want my mom to have hers right now."

"I don't believe that will be necessary. We would love to keep the one with Hannah's initials, if there's no one else in your family who would like to have it, but Hannah's doing so much better. . . . We don't need all three anymore."

"Okay," I say, relieved.

Dad steps in. "Mrs. Layton, we'll call you when we're more certain of the travel plans. There will be four of them driving down—my sister-in-law, Susan, her two oldest children, and Kate. Are you sure you don't mind having that many extra people in your home?"

"Please, call me Melanie, and, no, I don't mind at all. People have been incredibly kind to us throughout Hannah's illness. It will be wonderful to be on the giving end of things again. We'll look forward to having them."

The week drags on. It's weird to have Mom gone for so long. She and Dad have taken weekend vacations in the past, but she's never been gone for more than a few days. Dad goes to visit her Tuesday evening, and returns looking sad, tired, and lonely. I realize that I'm glad hospital rules prohibit me from visiting her.

Dad grabbed carryout from a Mexican restaurant on his way home, and we all help unpack the chips, salsa, queso dip, tacos, and burritos before taking our seats around the table.

"How's Mom?" I finally ask, tired of the tense silence.

"She's okay. They've started her on some medication to help balance out her mood, and she's . . . well, she's not herself. But she did seem a little bit happier. She said that she had a couple of group therapy sessions today, and met with her counselor privately as well. I had a chance to talk with her caseworker, and he thinks she'll be ready to come home in two to three weeks."

None of us knows what to say to this news, so silence falls around the table again.

"I got an A on my algebra test," I say, hoping to lighten the mood.

Dad gives me a small smile. "That's great, hon."

Gwen pipes up. "I got an A on my history test!"

"Good job, sweetheart," Dad turns the same half smile to Gwen.

Paul doesn't say anything, even though all eyes are on him. Finally, Dad ventures, "Paul, how's school going for you?"

"Okay."

"Have you had any tests recently?" Dad queries.

"Yeah. I didn't do so well."

"Mom usually helps him with studying," I say.

"Oh." Now Dad has a guilty look on his face. "Well, do you have a test tomorrow? We could work on it after dinner," Dad offers hopefully.

"No. But I do have a math worksheet that was really hard. You could probably check that," Paul allows.

Dad sits back in his seat and runs a tired hand over his face. "I'm sorry, kids. I know I'm a lousy substitute for your mom. I don't even know everything she did, and even if I *had* the whole list in front of me, I still don't think I could pull it off." He closes his eyes, and pinches the bridge of his nose. "I'll try to do better. Please just . . . let me know when I'm missing something, okay?"

"Okay, Dad. We will. And Gwen and I can help Paul too, can't we, Gwen?"

Gwen looks slightly horrified, but nods her head, "Yes, we can help him," she says, rather grudgingly.

"And next week will be spring break, so that will be easier. No homework or tests to worry about." I say brightly.

"Thanks, girls. I appreciate all your help."

His gratitude fills me with warmth. Life really stinks right now, but it's good to be able to help.

Finally, Saturday morning finds me, Evelyn, Dylan, and Aunt Susan piled into Mom's SUV, heading out of Indianapolis toward Pensacola, Florida. Even though I know we'll only be there for one night, I'm still looking forward to warmer weather. Winter seems to have come back to Indiana these last several days, and I'm hoping that maybe we can spend at least a few minutes on a real beach. I'd love to see the Gulf of Mexico, hear the rush of the waves, and feel the sand between my toes.

Evelyn and I chatter excitedly at first, but pretty soon the drone of the road beneath the car and the boring passage of flat, empty cornfields lull us into quiet. I finished the first book in the trilogy I was reading last week, and am making progress on the sequel. As our car eats up the miles between Indianapolis and Pensacola, I feel as though I'm leaving behind the unrest of the past year, and I feel slightly guilty for leaving Dad, Gwen, and Paul to deal with it alone. I know it's only a couple of days, but who will cook for them? Who will do the laundry? Who will load and unload the dishwasher? These are all responsibilities that have fallen to me as the oldest. As we drive, I look up from my book, stare at all the farmland and imagine coming home to an emaciated family that hasn't eaten for days, yet is nonetheless surrounded by dirty dishes.

I shake myself, realizing just how silly my thoughts are. Dad is perfectly capable of taking care of the house and his own children for a couple of days. It does feel good to be needed though. Part of me hopes that, when I come home, they will fall all over themselves, begging me to make Johnny Marzetti again.

Two hours into the trip, we celebrate passing from Indiana into Kentucky, peering down at the Ohio River from the giant bridge that crosses between the two states. We stop for lunch in southern Kentucky, and soon enjoy the rolling green hills of Tennessee. Two short hours later, we're in Alabama, and I am sure that the trip must be coming to a close. The drive wasn't nearly as bad as I had expected. Little do I know that Alabama is the world's longest state—or so it seems. Five hours later, we're still driving, but just when I think the trip will never end, I see a "Welcome to Florida" sign. Shortly after that, we begin to see the bustle of the suburbs of Pensacola.

Hannah's dad is in the navy, and they live near the naval base. We travel along the beach road briefly, before pulling off into a quiet, unassuming neighborhood. Hannah's house is a single-story ranch, painted a tropical peach color, with a palm tree in the front yard and evergreens draping their branches over the house from the back. We're not even out of the car when a woman emerges from the front door, a young girl clinging close at her side. The woman has long brown hair, pulled back in a ponytail, and wears a flowered skirt with a matching pink t-shirt.

The little girl, who must be Hannah, has short, curly brown hair that frames an adorable face with huge blue eyes. Her hands are stained with blue, and there are smudges of blue across her forehead and under her nose. We must have interrupted an art project.

The woman holds out her hand to Aunt Susan as she climbs from the driver's seat. "Hi, you must be Susan," she says warmly. "I'm Melanie. It's so nice to meet you."

"Hi, Melanie. Nice to meet you, as well. And I'll bet this is Hannah," Aunt Susan crouches down to get a better look at the young girl.

"Yep, this is Hannah," her mother puts a hand lovingly on the little girl's head, ruffling her curls with a smile, then looks expectantly at me, Evelyn, and Dylan.

"Hi, I'm Kate," I say, "and this is my cousin Evelyn, and this is Dylan. He's my cousin too," I finish awkwardly.

Melanie shakes each of our hands, murmuring polite greetings.

"Come in, come in. You must be exhausted after the long drive. My husband can get your bags out of the car. He should be home any minute." She ushers us into the comfortable little house. "I have some lemonade and cookies ready for you, and lasagna in the oven."

I smile, remembering her father's comment about his wife—her mother—always having lemonade and cookies ready for visitors. There's something sweet about remembering someone you love that way.

Melanie shows us into the living room, which holds an overstuffed sofa and loveseat, along with an armchair. Evelyn sits on the loveseat, and I sink down next to her. Aunt Susan and Dylan take the sofa.

Melanie sits in the armchair, leaning forward toward us, and her air of warm welcome slips. Her knee begins to bob up and down, and she wrings her hands nervously. "I'm"— she licks her lips—"I'm afraid I have some news. Some *bad* news."

Evelyn and I glance between each other and my heart begins a quick staccato in my chest. I don't like the sound of this.

"I didn't even think to ask Hannah for the bead until just a little bit ago," Melanie confides. "When I did, she told me that she gave one of the beads to her friend at the hospital. Her friend's been really sick, and is scheduled for surgery on Monday. We've spent a lot of time with this family. We had told them about the beads, and realized that one of the beads had Tara's initials on it. We went to visit her yesterday, and I guess while I was talking with Tara's mom . . . well, Hannah wanted to give her friend something that she thought might help her." Melanie presses her lips together and looks me in the eye. My heart sinks. I know what's coming next. "It's your mom's bead. Hannah doesn't have it anymore. She gave it to Tara."

I sit very still in my seat, not daring to move. I feel everyone's gaze on me, waiting to see my reaction. I squeeze my eyes shut, wishing this would all just go away. The room is quiet. Too quiet. I feel a tear slip past my clenched eyelids and slide down my cheek.

Evelyn pats my knee awkwardly, but I still don't open my eyes. I hear the sound of Aunt Susan rising from her spot on the sofa, then the click of her shoes across the tile floor. I open my eyes when I feel her hands on my knees and find her crouched in front of me. She looks deep into my eyes, sympathy etched across her face. I ask her the question that's circling around my head.

"Why? Why does it always have to be for someone *else*?" Aunt Susan gathers me into her arms as my chin wobbles and the tears start to fall in earnest.

Chapter Seventeen

I'm aware that I'm making a complete fool of myself, crying on Aunt Susan's shoulder in front of everyone. At the moment though, I don't really care, and taking these long moments to cry gives me time to digest what I've just learned without having to respond in any real way.

As I begin to calm down, my thoughts come into focus and I know that I've got to say something. I could demand that we go get the bead—*right now*. It's what I really want to do, after all, and a big part of me is mentally tallying all of the reasons why it would be okay to do just that.

Then I envision the cutest little girl you can imagine, with light brown hair framing a face filled with big brown eyes and an adorable bow of a mouth. I see her hooked up to wires and tubes, and I hear the beep, beep, beep of machines that are monitoring her breathing and heart rate, and keeping her alive. I imagine myself stomping into the room, a spoiled sixteen-year-old, an overgrown child, compared to the wise young girl in the bed. I see myself holding out my hand, demanding that she give me the bead—a bead that was given to her as a gift, a gift of innocent caring and love, a gift meant to calm her fears and give her hope for healing.

A gift that I can't possibly take away from this little girl.

Even while recognizing that, I still grasp at straws. *Maybe we could stay until Monday, and get it after her surgery?* I pose the question to myself.

No. She will need time to heal. Weeks, maybe even months. We don't even know what's wrong with her. Says my kinder, gentler side.

Maybe we could have a new one made, just like the other one, and give that to her? My childish, demanding side says—my I-want-what-I-want-and-I-want-it-now side.

No, it just wouldn't be the same, and you know it. There's that nobler side of me again.

The tears are gone now, and Aunt Susan releases me from her embrace, sitting back on her knees. She looks at me with concern and love.

I give her a watery smile, wiping my eyes with my sweatshirt sleeve. "It's okay." I manage to say. Then, "I could use a few minutes alone, though. Is it okay if I take a walk?"

Aunt Susan gives my forearms a gentle squeeze. "Of course, sweetie."

Melanie adds in a quiet voice, "The neighborhood's just a big loop. If you stay on this main street, you'll find your way back, no problem."

When I stand to leave, Hannah comes scampering into the room, holding a large piece of paper in her little hands. I hadn't even realized that she had left us when we sat down in the living room, but I'm guessing she must have gone to finish that art project. Splashes of silver and yellow have been added to the blue stains on her hands, and her shirt has a rather large splotch of green spilt down the front. When she sees me watching her, she slows to a walk, and casts her eyes at the floor. She approaches and gives me her paper, which I now see is soaked in paint.

Hannah glances up at me briefly, before looking at her feet again. "I'm sorry," she mumbles.

I study the painting by this little four-year-old artist. I recognize the blue sky, with a bright shining sun, and green grass below. There's a figure on the left hand side of the painting, wearing a blue gown, with what appears to be blue hair. On the right hand side, there are three stick figures, one tall, the other two smaller, all holding hands. They're wearing pink skirts, so they must all be girls. The taller one stands in the middle, with the two smaller ones on either side, each holding a circle—a necklace—in their free hand. One of the necklaces bears a single bead. The other bears two.

I sit back down in my seat on the sofa and study the painting. A tear drops onto the paper. "It's beautiful," I whisper, and give the little girl my best, watery smile.

She leans on my knee and begins to point out the figures. "That's me, and that's Tara," she says, pointing first to the girl with brown hair, then to the one with blond. Now, pointing to the taller figure, she says, "That's you. I couldn't finish it till I saw you to see what color your hair was." She looks at my blue jeans and blue sweatshirt and says, "I already painted the skirt," clearly disappointed by her lack of realism.

Next she points to the woman dressed in blue. "That's the Blessed Mother," she says, proudly. "She was always with me at the hospital, after Granddaddy gave me the necklace."

Startled, I look up at her mom. I hadn't known they were Catholic. Melanie's eyes have teared up, and she fingers the cross at her neck. She shakes her head and whispers, "We're not Catholic." She clears her throat and says more clearly, "I don't know where it all came from, but after Dad gave her the beads, she started talking about a woman, dressed in blue, who was with her at the hospital, whenever we couldn't be there, and sometimes even when we were. Then one day, she started calling her 'the Blessed Mother.' It didn't make sense, until Dad told me where the beads had actually come from . . ." she shakes her head in disbelief. "It still doesn't make sense, really, does it?" she whispers.

I shake my head, and smile at Hannah. "I love it," I tell her. I feel the tears coming on again, and I pull Hannah into a hug. She comes to me willingly, and puts her arms around my shoulders as I bury my face in her curly ringlets. "Thank you," I whisper into her hair.

Hannah nods her head and squeezes me tightly.

After several moments, Hannah sits on my lap and snuggles into my chest. All thoughts of a walk leave me for the time being, and I simply enjoy the warmth of this sweet, loving, innocent child. I think of all that she's been through in such a short life, and I wish that I could give her more than just this nearness.

Finally, Hannah looks up at me. "My mommy says that your mommy is sick." I nod my head. "I gave her bead to Tara, but I still have two beads left. I want to give your mommy one of them."

"It's okay, Hannah. I have one I can give my mom. I want you to keep both of those. Who knows? You may meet another child who needs one of the beads."

Hannah looks relieved, and looks up at me with a blinding smile. "Okay. 'Cause there is a boy I met, Leo. Leo starts with L, right?"

"That's right," I say encouragingly.

"My other bead has an L on it, so I thought maybe I could give it to him."

"I think that would be wonderful, Hannah."

Having gained my approval for her plan, Hannah jumps from my lap and runs off to play, or perhaps to create another painting. The room is silent for a moment.

"I think I'll take that walk now, if it's okay?" I ask.

Melanie nods her head, and Aunt Susan responds, "Of course, hon. Don't be gone too long, though, okay?"

Walking out the front door, I revel in the feel of the warm air, grateful for the break from the still-cold early spring in Indiana. I turn right and follow the main street, as Melanie had advised. Feeling an unfamiliar bulk in my jeans pocket, I realize that my rosary is still there, where I shoved it after we prayed at the beginning of our drive, for safe travels. I pull it out and enjoy the feel of the beads in my fingers. I run my thumb over Christ's body, on the crucifix, and find myself beginning the prayer.

Half an hour later, I realize that I'm a few houses down from Melanie and Hannah's home. I've finished the Rosary, and have been lost in thought for several minutes. Once again, the prayer has left me feeling much calmer, and I'm able to reason through the events of the day—and even the past few weeks.

I realize now that I need to trust in God that my mom will get better. That, while the beads do seem to provide some special grace, like Uncle Joseph said, they are not the *only* way that a person can be helped or healed. My mom can be helped through my prayers, through my faith, and through the prayers of others.

In fact, I realize, perhaps just hearing the stories of healings that have taken place will be helpful to Mom. Knowing that Grandma's death does not appear to have been in vain, but instead that her prayers—for Emma, Hannah, and James—have been answered. And her prayers for us are being answered, as well.

As I walk, I think about these people whom I have met in the past few weeks, and I thank God that they've come into my life. Each of their stories has become very important to me, and I have felt an extraordinary connection with Hannah, Emma and James, and even Chelsea, Beth, and Mr. Billings. It's as though all of us whose lives have been touched by these very special beads now possess a unique bond with each other.

I thank God for the lives that he has saved, for the miraculous grace flowing forth from these beads, through the prayers and intercession of the Blessed Mother and, presumably, my grandmother.

I think of my own faith and prayer life. Five weeks ago, even though I attended Catholic school and used to go to Mass every Sunday, God was really just an empty idea, floating out there as some reassurance that a higher being did exist. Today, God has become central to my existence, Christ has become present to me as my savior, and his Blessed Mother has become the key to growing in my friendship with him.

I remember the dream I had when this all began. The field, with the plants trying to hold me down, the sea of beads, and being carried across it to arrive near Grandma and the woman, whom I now know to be the Blessed Mother. That sea of beads must surely be each prayer that Grandma prayed for me and for the members of our family. Those prayers held so much power, that they have, indeed, delivered me at the feet of a heavenly mother I never knew.

I stop walking, and gaze at the rosary in my hand. Rolling a bead between my thumb and forefinger, it hits me.

These beads *do* possess a special power. But it's not magic, and it's not the stuff of some sci-fi story. The power of a single bead lies entirely in the power of a single prayer.

And every single prayer holds awesome power—the power of God, who listens, and heals, and loves.

A single bead. A single prayer. Unlimited grace and possibilities.

Chapter Eighteen

Eventually, I look up from the bead in my hand and smile at the world around me, a world fresh with faith and hope. The sun is setting in front of me, and I realize that I've been gone much longer than I intended. I figure I must have walked right past Melanie's house in my reverie, and so I turn around to head in the opposite direction, hoping that I haven't gotten more than halfway around the second time.

Five minutes later, I'm approaching the house, and Aunt Susan is sitting on the step of the front porch. She, too, holds rosary beads in her hand, leaving me little doubt as to what she's been doing outside by herself.

As I amble up the step, Aunt Susan looks up at me with an inquisitive smile. I return the smile, and she releases her breath. She scoots over and pats the step next to her. I sit down and stare pensively at the flowers on the other side of the walk.

Aunt Susan breaks the silence. "I've been thinking," she says, holding the rosary up out of her lap. "Well, I was praying, and I guess I got a bit sidetracked. You remember Uncle Joseph's story about Blessed Mother Teresa's rosary, and how it seemed to work miracles for the people who had it? Obviously, not every set of rosary beads is connected to miracles. That particular rosary must have been special because of the holy woman who prayed on it."

That makes sense, so I nod my head. Aunt Susan continues, "There's no denying that something special is going on with these beads, too. But just like Mother Teresa's rosary, those beads are showing us the power of the many prayers that were prayed on them and the faith of the woman who prayed them. Maybe Grandma has found a special place at the Blessed Mother's side. I can picture the two of them up there, bending Jesus' ear with the prayer requests of anyone who holds these beads, don't you think?"

I nod slowly. Uncle Joseph said something similar to that a couple of weeks ago.

"You've got a bead, so surely they're up there praying for you, right? And I would imagine that your number one prayer right now is for your mom. What struck me is this: they've given you everything you need to help your mom, it's just taken a little bit of time to recognize it."

Now she's lost me, so I look at her quizzically.

"Have you ever wondered what's *really* wrong with your mom?" Aunt Susan asks.

"She's depressed. Isn't that it?" I answer uncertainly.

"Well, yes, that's true. But *why* is she depressed? When did it all start?"

"It started when Grandma's plane crashed. And it got really bad after the memorial a few weeks ago, and even worse after she found out about my bead."

"Right," Aunt Susan says. "So, she's depressed because her mother died. If that's all there is to it, though, why aren't all of the siblings depressed? Sure, they all miss their mother, but they've all managed to go through the grieving process in the normal, healthy way. Oh, it seemed to take a little longer for Liz than it did for Mary Ellen, and it was different for Joseph than it was for David, but they've all accepted your grandma's death and managed to get on with their lives. So, why did it hit your mom so much harder? Why hasn't *she* been able to move forward?"

I shrug. I guess I hadn't really thought that far.

Aunt Susan turns on the step so she can look me in the eye. "It's *faith*, Kate. Faith. Mary Ellen, Joseph, Liz, David, Matthew and Jonathan: they all have very strong faith. That's what has brought them through this. They *know* that your grandma was a good, holy woman, and when she died they *knew* that God would be good to her. Sure, they've offered up countless rosaries and Masses for the eternal rest of her soul, but they've had faith—all along—that, even though we can never know exactly where a soul goes when it leaves this earth, their mother would spend eternity with God in heaven, eventually. And they've been able to celebrate Grandma's life, even as they mourn their loss. Your mom . . ." Aunt Susan looks away from me, trying to find the right words, "well, your mom hasn't really grown in her faith, at least not since I've known her. Your Uncle David remembers that Teresa seemed to turn away from her beliefs when she went to college. She left the Church and she never really came back. So, she hasn't had a strong relationship with God to help pull her through this."

Aunt Susan looks at me like she's solved the world's greatest mystery, and I ought to be jumping for joy, but I still don't get it.

"Great," I say, a bit perturbed. "So how does any of this give us the magical answer to all of Mom's problems? How is talking about her *relationship with God* going to help make her better?"

Hearing the irritation in my voice, Aunt Susan puts her hand on my knee. "The *beads*, Kate. They provide the answer. Has your mom heard all these amazing stories?" I shake my head. "I think she should. You know, miracles serve more than one purpose. Sure, they offer healing, protection, and grace. But miracles also help build *faith*. The blessings connected with Grandma's rosary beads assure us that your grandmother's prayers are still being answered. It's the whole package—right there in front of us—if we just recognize it as such."

"So you're telling me that Mom's going to get better overnight if I tell her all these stories?" I ask, incredulous.

"No, but I think that the stories do seem rather miraculous, and that knowing about them might help her through the grieving process. Maybe she'd be able to trust that her mom really *is* in a better place. Maybe she'd be open to rebuilding her faith, so that she can lean on *Christ* to get her through the rest of the grieving that she needs to do."

I nod my head, as it starts to become clear to me. The hope that sprouted in me as I was praying the Rosary on my walk blossoms and takes life, as I begin to understand how all of this can help Mom. I think through everything that Aunt Susan's said, and my face breaks into a huge grin.

"Aunt Susan, you're a genius. I think you're on to something," I say, before giving her a huge hug.

Aunt Susan hugs me back, and I enjoy the comforting warmth of this woman who I realize is almost another mom to me. I giggle a bit, thinking about the fact that I now have four moms—my own mom, of course; Aunt Mary Ellen and Aunt Susan, who have both become such a big part of my life; and the Blessed Mother. It seems like more than any one girl should have, and my heart swells with knowledge of how blessed I actually am.

Aunt Susan laughs a bit as she hears my giggle, "What are you laughing about?" she asks, clearly relieved that I seem to be in such a good mood.

"Nothing," I smile back. "It's just . . ." I slide a glance up at her, "that God's pretty amazing, isn't he?"

"Yes," she agrees, with another quick squeeze, "he sure is."

Chapter Nineteen

When we walk into the house, my mouth waters at the smell of lasagna. The dining room table is set, and everyone seems to be waiting for us. It hits me that I've been terribly rude to Melanie—walking into their house, bawling my eyes out, and taking off for forty-five minutes when I knew that dinner was nearly ready.

I apologize awkwardly, but Melanie assures me that it's fine and she understands. Then she introduces me to her husband and invites us to take our seats at the table.

We all get to know each other over dinner. I learn that Hannah is a precocious little girl who has already begun to read. She loves to dance and sing—something we have in common, even if she is twelve years younger than I am. Melanie used to teach elementary school, until Hannah got so sick, but is now enjoying being a stay-at-home mom— especially, she tells me with a twinkle in her eye, since they just recently found out that they're expecting another child in November.

Hannah's dad seems to be a man of few words. He doesn't say much during dinner, but is clearly very gentle and loving with both Hannah and Melanie. After she's finished, Hannah climbs up into his lap, twines her arms around his neck, and rests her head on his chest. I think of all this family's been through, and how wonderful it must be for them to enjoy a normal family dinner without the cloud of a life-threatening illness hanging over their heads.

We all agree that it would be nice to go down to the beach before bed. I ask Aunt Susan if I can call Dad first, and of course she agrees. He picks up on the first ring.

"Hi, Dad."

"Hi, sweetie. How was your drive?"

"Good." I stop, realizing that's not true. "Long and boring," I correct.

Dad chuckles. "Yeah, I imagine it was. And you get to turn around and do it again tomorrow, huh?"

"Yeah, but we're going to the beach for a little bit tonight," I say, my tone brightening.

"Mmmmm. That sounds great. Will you bring me back some sand?"

I smile. "Sure, I can do that." I hesitate, seeking the right words for the question I've called to ask.

"Dad?"

"Yes, honey?"

"I know that the—the facility that Mom's at doesn't allow kids to visit, but do you think they would make an exception if it might help the—the patient get better?" I stumble over the hard words, the ones that identify my mom as a person who's sick.

"Well, the information that they gave me did say that they make exceptions occasionally. I take it you got the bead?"

"No," I answer. "I think I got something better."

We leave the Laytons' house at six thirty the next morning. Aunt Susan found a church that offers Mass at seven, so we're headed there before hitting the road. This took me by surprise; my family never goes to Mass on vacation, and I didn't pack Mass clothes. Of course, the church is filled with old people, all dressed in their Sunday best, and I find myself tugging at the bright blue t-shirt which isn't quite long enough to cover the grey leggings I'm wearing underneath. Evelyn and Dylan came better prepared, and she gives me an apologetic look as we sit down, smoothing her skirt over her lap.

Apparently, they don't do music for the insanely early Masses, so Mass is quick, and my embarrassment is limited.

After Mass, Evelyn and I find a park bench outside to wait while Dylan and Aunt Susan talk to the priest and take pictures of the church for some project that Dylan's working on for religion class. Evelyn gives me a doleful look. "I'm sorry. I should have warned you. We *always* go to Mass on Sunday, whether we're in Chicago or Timbuktu. Mom *finds* a church."

"It's okay. I should have known," I reassure her. "Besides, it was kind of cool. They do exactly the same stuff at this church that we do at home, or at St. Joan of Arc."

"Yeah, I always used to complain about going to Mass on vacation, but now I sort of like it. Each church is a little bit different, but underneath it all, the Mass is the same, and the people are usually really friendly." Evelyn thinks for a moment, then glances sideways at me. "You okay with letting Hannah's friend keep the bead?" she asks.

I shrug, once again putting my fingers on my own bead. "Yeah. I felt a lot better after I took that walk last night. I prayed a Rosary and felt really calm and hopeful afterward. Then, your mom and I talked and she really put it into perspective. Basically, she said that Mom doesn't need the *bead*, she needs *faith*, and it's the *stories of the beads* that will help her find faith again." I bite my lip, wondering now if it can really be that simple. "Does that make any sense?" I ask Evelyn, hoping for validation, but fearing that she'll tell me it's crazy.

Evelyn thinks for a minute, twisting her hair around her finger and pulling it over her lips as she ponders this idea. Finally, she begins to nod her head. "Yeah. Yeah, that does make sense." She smiles and reaches over for a hug. As we pull back apart, she says, "Well, I guess it's too bad we drove all the way down here for nothing."

"It wasn't for nothing," I respond. "I think I needed faith, too, and meeting Hannah, spending time with them, hearing about how she got better for no reason, and the doctors can't figure it out . . . I needed to see it for myself before I try to share it with Mom."

Seeing movement out of the corner of my eye, I glance back toward the church. Aunt Susan and Dylan are headed our way, finished with their business. We walk together to the car, then settle in for the long trip home.

My feet feel like lead as we approach the reception desk. Dad never mentioned that Mom was in a *hospital*. Somehow, calling it a "facility" made it sound so much nicer, and I wasn't prepared for the sterility that struck me when the automatic doors gave us entry into the hospital's Stress Center. The walls are white, with a few bland pictures scattered about. The furniture is that ugly blue plastic stuff you find at every hospital, and the smell . . . well, it's that awful mixture of sterilizer, bodily fluids, and goodness only knows what else.

The thought of Mom being stuck in this place makes me shudder. We've definitely had our differences lately, but I wouldn't wish this on my worst enemy.

The lady behind the reception desk is friendly, though. When Dad tells her we're here to see Teresa Roberts, and that the doctors have made an exception for my visit, she refers to the computer before smiling and motioning for us to sit down.

The pleather chairs hold no appeal, so I wander over to the windows and look outside, where a few tulips are breaking through the soil. I'm just making bets with myself on what color they're going to be, when I hear the doors open. I turn to see a man dressed, not in the hospital scrubs that I was expecting, but in khaki pants and a navy blue dress shirt.

"Mr. Roberts, good to see you," he says, shaking Dad's hand, "and, you must be Katelyn," he says, turning to me with a friendly smile and a warm handshake.

I nod my head, avoiding his eyes and looking at his name badge instead. It's hanging backward, so rather than identifying who he is I squint to try to read the hospital's mission statement.

"I'm Dr. Becker. I've been spending a lot of time with your mom, working to help her get home to you as soon as possible," he explains.

"Oh. Nice to meet you," I say, remembering my manners and forcing my gaze up to his.

"Katelyn, your dad explained that you have something to tell your mom that you believe might help her get better. If you don't mind, I'd like to talk with you about that before we meet with your mom. She's doing really well. We want to make sure, before we introduce anything new, that it won't upset her in any way. Sometimes things that we *think* will be of benefit can actually end up *hurting* more than they help. Do you understand?"

I nod my head again, suddenly feeling even more nervous. Will they keep me from seeing Mom? I've come this far, I don't want to have to wait until she gets home to tell her. And what if they say all these amazing stories are harmful, and I shouldn't tell her at all? I panic.

Dr. Becker uses his badge to activate the automatic doors, which open onto a hallway with rooms off either side. I'm pleasantly surprised to see that, here, the walls are painted a warm tan color, and the artwork is a little more colorful. We pass what looks like a living room area, where people are playing games, reading magazines, and watching TV. A little more of my horror melts away as I notice the comfortable couches, scattered pillows, and people who actually look completely normal.

Finally, he ushers us into an office, complete with messy desk and shelves lined with books. A picture of him with what must be his wife and two kids sits on one shelf, in front of a book title that takes a moment to register. *The Bible*. Then I notice a picture of the Blessed Mother, framed, on the wall beside the window. Perhaps I've found an ally?

Dr. Becker settles into his chair, and leans forward with his arms resting on his desk. He clasps his hands, looks at me, and says, "So, Katelyn, tell me what's brought you here."

I take a deep breath and begin my tale.

Twenty minutes later, Dr. Becker leans back in his seat, puts his hands behind his head, and stares up toward the ceiling, seemingly lost in thought. After a few moments, he looks at me kindly. When I see the sympathy in his eyes, I fear that it's all over. His words do nothing to encourage me.

"Katelyn, it was brave of you to come here. You must be a very strong young woman. Your mom is in a fragile place right now. She's doing much better, and has made significant improvement in the last week. I'm not at liberty to discuss the details with you, but I can tell you this. Your story has the potential to cause your mother to relapse. In fact, I believe that her knowledge of this bead situation triggered the worsening of her condition over the last month or so, which led to her need to stay with us here."

Every word is a nail in the coffin of my hope, and my eyes fill with tears. Dad reaches over to squeeze my hand as Dr. Becker continues, his face a blur through the haze of my tears.

"However, it doesn't sound as though your mom knows the whole story. She only knows that you found your bead and a few others, and that you're working to find still more. She doesn't know about the wonderful things that seem to be associated with these beads." He sits forward, leaning on the arm of his chair. "This theory your aunt proposed, about your mom's faith and accepting that your grandmother is truly in a better place, well, it does have some merit."

I hadn't realized that I was holding my breath, until I let it out in a loud exhale. I lean forward, "So, can I see her?"

"Well, Katelyn," he says, slowly, "we don't know *how* your mom will respond. You would need to be prepared for every possibility. Best-case scenario, your mom realizes that you're here to help her, listens to your story, and gives it serious consideration. Maybe it would help in her recovery, but it's not going to be an instantaneous reaction, rather one that happens over months or even years."

"That doesn't sound too bad, Dr. Becker," I say.

"But that isn't the only possibility," he continues guard-edly. "In the worst case, your mom could be unable to reconcile the emotions that she has in regards to this whole situation. She could get angry when you tell her the story. She could get more depressed. It's impossible to say.

"Mr. Roberts," Dr. Becker says, turning to my dad, "it's important for you to understand that this could have a negative impact on your wife, *and* on your daughter as well. If Teresa responds in a negative way, that could be an awful lot for a teenager to deal with emotionally. As your wife's therapist, I'm open to exploring this avenue, in the hope that it would be helpful to her. If I were counseling your daughter, however, I might advise against it." He pauses, then raises his eyebrows and asks Dad, "What's your thought on the matter?"

⌖

Two days later, I find myself sitting in a small meeting room at the Stress Center. Dad and I are seated on one side of the small table that dominates the room. He drums his fingers on its surface, while I sit on the edge of my seat, staring at the framed floral print on the wall across from me. Two chairs remain unoccupied, awaiting the arrival of my mom and Dr. Becker.

Dad tried to talk me out of doing this, and made me wait two days to make sure that I was ready for whatever may happen. Bottom line is, I don't feel like I've got much to lose. Plus, I've prayed about it—*a lot*—and I feel like this is what I need to do. So, here we are.

The door opens. I feel myself tense, and the sound of Dad's fingers tapping on the table stops. It's been nearly two weeks since I last saw Mom, and months since she showed any affection for me. I'm not sure what to expect, and not sure what to do. So I stay in my seat as Dad rises to give her a hug and kiss.

I watch with interest to see how she will respond, and am reassured to see her hug him back, fiercely. When she comes to stand next to my chair, I rise and give her a half-hearted hug, only to find that she's squeezing me and doesn't seem to want to let go. Finally, I hug her back, sinking into her warmth and comfort, grateful for this small tenderness that is so long overdue. After several moments, she lets me go, then takes the chair beside me. Dr. Becker takes the one remaining chair, and looks expectantly at Mom.

"Kate," she begins, then clears her throat. "I've been doing a lot of thinking since I've come here, and I realize that I owe you an apology. I haven't been much of a mother to you in the last year or so, and for that I am very sorry. It's just . . ."

I don't want to hear her excuses or explanations, and hold up my hand to stop her. "Mom, it's okay. I'm fine," I lie. "I'm here because . . ." I search for the words, and finding none that seem suitable, I blurt out: "I'm here because Grandma sent me."

Mom jerks back, her face showing total surprise, before a shutter comes down over it and there's no emotion whatsoever. Dad coughs beside me, clearly shocked that I would come right out and say it like that. Dr. Becker leans forward, ready to come to the rescue, but I rush on before he can get a word out.

"Well, she did," I say, looking defiantly at the doctor and my dad. "But before you blow this off and decide not to listen to a word I say, let me start at the beginning." Taking a deep breath, I begin. It feels like I've told the story a million times now. Finding my bead on the day of Grandma's memorial, meeting Chelsea, and her friend Emma, the story of Emma's accident, and how she was miraculously uninjured. Then, talking to Roger Billings, and learning about Hannah and her amazing recovery. I tell her about Beth and her brother James, and the vision that he had that led to him overcoming his addiction. I tell her about our trip down to Florida to get her bead from little Hannah. All the while, Mom sits back in her chair, arms crossed over her chest, as though she doesn't believe it, or doesn't care. But I plow on, praying as I speak, whenever I pause, *Blessed Mother, Grandma, please help me.* I know that, without them, I'll never finish the story.

Somehow, I manage to ignore Mom's look of indifference, and pretend that I'm talking to someone who cares. "Mom, you should have seen little Hannah. She's the cutest thing. And she's so *healthy.* You'd never guess she'd ever been sick. And get this! She said that a woman was with her in the hospital, whenever her mom and dad couldn't be there. Mom," I lean forward, "she called the woman 'the Blessed Mother,'" I wait for my words to sink in before adding, "and *she's not even Catholic.*"

Mom's jaw tightens, and her gaze jumps away from mine. She glares resolutely at the same floral print that I stared at earlier, before she entered the room. My resolve begins to crack. Should I even keep going? I don't seem to be getting anywhere. The progress I thought we'd made—when she hugged me—all seems to be lost. We're right back to where we started, several weeks ago. I say another prayer, and keep going.

"Our whole reason for going down there was to get your bead. I thought . . . I thought maybe it would help you." Mom chews on her bottom lip. I wait a moment, thinking she might say something, but she doesn't, so I continue, "But Hannah gave your bead to her friend Tara from the hospital, who was really sick and going to have surgery on Monday. She thought it might help her." My heart races as I search for the words to share the latest news, which is so incredible. So unbelievable. So *miraculous.* There was a bunch of medical lingo that I didn't understand, and I look at Dad, my eyes pleading with him to take over for me.

Dad reads my cue, and jumps in, leaning on the table to get Mom's attention. She finally stops glaring at the flower on the wall and looks at him.

"Teresa, Hannah's mom called yesterday, as soon as she got the news. Tara's surgery was to remove a brain tumor. All the tests beforehand showed that it was wrapped around her brain stem, and the doctors were sure that they wouldn't be able to get all of it. They had hoped to get most of it, and then be able to treat the rest with chemo and radiation. Apparently, there was a very good chance that she might not even make it through the surgery." Dad clears his throat, and continues, "Teresa, you know I'm the least likely person to believe in this stuff, but"—he glances between me and the doctor, then back to Mom—"this is amazing, Teresa. It just can't be a coincidence. When they went in, the tumor had shrunk down, to almost nothing, and they were able to get all of it. The doctors were stunned. There's no explanation, they say. The doctors say it's a miracle. The little girl—Tara? When she woke up afterwards, she asked for the lady in blue, the one that held her hand and loved her so much."

No one speaks. I listen to the soft ticking of the clock on the wall, and hear the sound of someone walking down the hall outside the closed door. Mom shifts her eyes away from Dad, and looks instead at the hands clenched tightly in her lap. A tear splashes onto her thumb.

"Mom," I say quietly, "I think all of this is happening because Grandma prayed so, so many times on each of those beads. I know it sounds crazy, but I think Grandma's prayers are being answered with these miracles. But I think there's something else, another reason . . . Mom, I think it's because she prayed for *you*. I think she wants you to know that she's okay, that she's in a better place," I gulp, wishing I hadn't used that cliché, but knowing that it's true. "I think she wants you to *believe*." I finish, and sit back in my seat, as once again silence fills the room.

I sit there, waiting for Mom to respond, waiting for her to say *something, anything*. But she doesn't. She just pushes back her chair, opens the door, and walks out of the room.

It's been three long days, days spent beating myself up, wishing I hadn't gone, that I hadn't said anything to Mom. Clearly, it didn't help a bit, and maybe it only made things worse. I wonder if I'll ever have a real *mom* again, or if I'll be stuck for the rest of my life with this shell of a woman.

Tomorrow is Easter Sunday. Aunt Mary Ellen picked me and Gwen up on Thursday to shop for Easter dresses and new shoes. The family celebration is planned for Aunt Susan's house, but I don't feel much like celebrating.

Aunt Liz is in town. Evelyn and I gave her bead to her this morning over breakfast. She cried and hugged both of us, and listened to Evelyn share the stories of all the miracles that have happened. I couldn't bring myself to add anything more than the occasional weak smile. It was good to see Aunt Liz so happy, but at the same time it only made me more angry that my own mom doesn't seem to believe the stories.

Around noon, I'm eating yet another peanut butter and jelly sandwich when the phone rings. Gwen picks it up, then yells down the stairs, "Kate! It's for you!"

"Hello?" I say, putting the phone to my ear.

"Hi, Kate, it's Aunt Mary Ellen. I just visited your mom. She wants to see you, and asked me to bring you this afternoon. The doctor's already said it's okay."

My heart begins to race, and my hands get suddenly clammy. "What does she want?" I ask, afraid to hope that it's good news.

"She didn't say, sweetie, but she's doing much better today. There's a sparkle in her eyes that I haven't seen in ages. She *smiled*, Kate, really smiled, and she asked how you and Paul and Gwen are doing. I think what you told her helped. I think it *must* have." She pauses, then asks, "Can I come pick you up now? She seemed really anxious to see you."

I look down at my sweatpants and t-shirt, and run a hand through hair that I haven't washed in three days. Not really how I want to present myself to this new mom that Aunt Mary Ellen says has emerged. Nonetheless, if she's really doing better, and if she wants to see me . . . "Yeah. How soon will you be here?"

"Ten minutes."

I hang up the phone and run upstairs to change into something more presentable, something Mom would like. I find a blue skirt and white quarter sleeve shirt, and, after inspection shows that they're not too terribly wrinkly, I throw them on. I scrub my teeth and am still pulling the brush through my tangled hair when I hear Aunt Mary Ellen calling from the kitchen.

"Kate, are you ready?"

With one final yank of the hairbrush, I trip down the stairs and arrive, huffing a bit, in front of my aunt. I find Dad in the den to let him know where I'm going, ignoring his look of shock when he hears the news. I realize that I'm forgetting something, and race back up to my room. I grab the painting that Hannah had given me, tuck it into a folder to protect it, and cram the folder into my backpack. Finally, Aunt Mary Ellen and I are in the car, headed back to the Stress Center.

A friendly woman leads me to the same room where Dad and I met with Mom and Dr. Becker before. This time, they're already in there, waiting.

"Kate, I'm so glad you came," Mom sounds relieved as she stands and gives me a hug. This time it's quick and unsure, and I feel my hands grow clammy again, wondering where this is all headed.

Mom sits back down in her chair, and waits for me to sit before she begins.

"Kate, I told you last time you were here that I'm sorry. And I mean it. I *am* sorry. More than you can know. There's no excuse for how badly I've treated you this past year. But I want you to understand *why*—where I've been coming from—even though I know I've been terribly wrong, and there's really no excuse."

Mom takes a sip from the cup of water that's sitting on the table, and then takes a deep breath before beginning. "I don't know how to describe all the feelings I went through when Mom died. I loved her so much, yet in the last ten years, I hadn't been much of a daughter for her. When Dad died, I was angry with her because she seemed so okay with it. Oh, sure, she clearly missed him, but she would smile serenely and say how glad she was that he was out of pain, and that she trusted he would be in heaven when she got there. I thought it was just so *stupid*, so *ridiculous* . . . I wanted Dad back, and it made me mad when she said that wanting to keep him here, when he was in so much pain from the cancer, was selfish. So I spent most of those last two years being angry with Mom, and really wanting nothing to do with her. She was all wrapped up in her faith, always praying, always saying that Christ brought her through Dad's illness and death, and that he would bring her through anything she faced. I just didn't get it, and it just made me more and more angry.

"I wanted to try to get over being so mad at her, and the day before she left on her trip, I asked her to have breakfast with me. But she said that she couldn't. Her Rosary prayer group was meeting to pray for someone, and then they were having breakfast afterward. I felt hurt and got even more angry with her. I told her how stupid I thought she was for wasting so much time praying that ridiculous prayer. I told her that all of her prayers hadn't done a thing to help Dad, that it wouldn't help the person that she was praying for, and that it was just a way for a bunch of old ladies to feel like they were doing something productive when, in fact, they were just wasting time." Mom closes her eyes, pain etched across her face.

"The next day, she left on her trip, and there was the accident, and I never saw her again. Those were my last words to her. 'Mom, you're just wasting your time. You could do so much, and make such a difference, but instead you spend hours praying that ridiculous Rosary. You're a fool.'" My mom looks up from the water that she's been staring into, straight into my eyes, "I actually said those words, 'You're a fool.'" She shakes her head, then looks back down into her cup.

"You've always reminded me of her. You've got her eyes, and her mouth. I think your voice sounds like hers, and sometimes, when I hear you on the phone, I think for a moment that it's Mom." She looks at me again, "That's why I've been so distant from you this last year. I just couldn't bear it. You made me think of her, and I couldn't stand to think about her, and the way that I treated her. Your presence felt like a judgement against me. Then you found that bead"—she shakes her head and looks off into the corner—"and that was the last straw. It brought everything rushing back, and I just couldn't deal with it. I wanted you to just lay off the whole subject, to bury that bead and forget that it ever existed. But no, you didn't do that. You went looking for more." She gives a bitter chuckle, "You *had* to go looking for more.

"There's a crucifix that hangs in my room here. At first, I couldn't stand having it there. It was like Jesus was looking down at me, telling me what a terrible person I was, for being so cruel to my mom, and my own daughter. After you came on Wednesday, though, it changed. Suddenly, I started to remember things that I learned in school. 'Father, forgive them, for they know not what they do.' Jesus' words from the cross kept coming back to me, and I realized that he forgives me, and wants me to forgive myself. I thought about what you said, and I realized that Mom forgives me, too, and that she wants me to be happy."

Tears are streaming down her face now, and mine too. Mom continues, "I never stopped believing, you know? I believed in Jesus; I just didn't really want it to go any further than that. I didn't want to change my life or my ways because of him. That's what bugged me so much about Mom. Everything she *was*, was *all about Jesus*. I just didn't get it, and I'm still not sure that I do, but it's starting to make sense. And I know you're right, Kate. I know that Mom *is* in a better place, and it's just like her to just keep praying. Praying for people in need, and praying to give me a gentle nudge to get me back in line, to get me to believe what she's been trying to show me all along. Jesus is *real*. Mary is *real*. It's all *real*, and it's there for the taking, if only we open ourselves up to it."

Mom leans forward and grabs my hands where they lie on the table. "Thank you, Kate," she says emphatically, "Thank you for telling me all those wonderful and miraculous stories. I feel so much better. I feel so much more *hope*. I feel like I can accept your Grandma's death, and grandpa's too. I know Mom was right, with all she said when Dad died. I have to laugh, thinking about her up there orchestrating all of these things." She gives me a watery smile, and I find myself rising from my chair to give her a hug. Next thing I know, I'm sitting in her lap, even though I'm way too old to sit in my mom's lap anymore. But it feels so right, and we're hugging, and crying, and laughing, and reveling in this new *us*.

A long time later, we leave the room together. Dr. Becker asks a nurse to accompany us, and Mom and I walk hand in hand toward the waiting room. Before reaching the automatic doors, I remember Hannah's picture in my backpack. Pulling it out, I hand it to Mom.

"Hannah, the little girl in Florida, painted this for me. It's a picture of her and her friend Tara, with me and the Blessed Mother. I thought it might be something nice for you to have in your room."

Next, I reach behind my neck and unclasp the chain, then drop the bead into my palm.

"And," I say, holding the small treasure out to her, "I want you to have this, at least until you come home."

Mom cradles the bead in her hand and gives me a smile, tears once again welling in her eyes. Clasping me in another hug, she whispers, "Thank you, sweetheart. Thank you."

Turning back toward the waiting room doors, I notice that the nurse is staring at us with her mouth gaping open.

"Where—where did you get that?" she asks, pointing to the bead.

"It was my grandmother's," I answer.

"My—my niece found a bead just—just like that," the woman stammers. Looking at me with wide eyes, she adds, "You won't believe what happened. . . ."

Questions for Discussion

1. Why do you think Kate doesn't tell anyone in her family about the bead she finds on the day she first finds it?

2. After Kate finds the first bead, she and Evelyn conspire to go to another town to learn the story of Chelsea and Emma's bead. How might the story have changed if Kate and Evelyn had told their parents the truth to begin with?

3. Faith is both personal and individual. In Kate's large extended family, there are people who have strong faith, weak faith, and no faith. How does your family reflect this reality?

4. How does Kate's belief in God change over the course of the story? How do the events of the story affect Kate's dad and what he believes?

5. On page 127, Kate says that she used to believe the Rosary was "stupid," and that it was "useless to spend twenty minutes praying." What was your opinion of the Rosary or the Blessed Virgin Mary before reading this book? Has reading Kate's story made you change or rethink that opinion in any way?

6. This story is a work of fiction. Other than the theology shared by Father Joseph, where do you think there might be grains of truth underlying the story?

7. Kate experiences very powerful answers to prayer, but they aren't always the answers she wanted or expected. Share a time when you've had an answered prayer, or a time that a prayer seemed to go unanswered. Was it simply answered in a manner you hadn't expected? What can you learn from that unexpected answer?

8. Kate's family experienced a traumatic loss when their grandmother died. What might they have done differently to help Kate's mother, and the family as a whole, cope more effectively?

9. Kate's grandmother was someone who inspired faith in others. How did she do this? What actions or qualities do you see in others which inspire you to grow closer to God?

Stephanie Engelman is a wife and mother of five whose degree in psychology only partially prepared her for the insanity of a small house filled with a big family. She is a convert to Catholicism and feels led to share her love for Christ and his Church with others through the gifts and talents God has given her. However, she never imagined she'd write fiction until inspiration hit in the form of a social media message from a complete stranger. What started as a wry prayer turned into Stephanie's first novel. She hopes it will lead many to a deeper connection with God, their faith, and the Blessed Mother. You can follow Stephanie at facebook.com/s.engelman.author.

Author photo by Char Cota

TEEN
Pauline

Who: The Daughters of St. Paul

What: Pauline Teen—linking your life to Jesus Christ and his Church

When: 24/7

Where: All over the world and on www.pauline.org

Why: Because our life-long passion is to witness to God's amazing love for all people!

How: Inspiring lives of holiness through: Apps, digital media, concerts, websites, social media, videos, blogs, books, music albums, radio, media literacy, DVDs, ebooks, stores, conferences, bookfairs, parish exhibits, personal contact, illustration, vocation talks, photography, writing, editing, graphic desi
marketing

BOOKS & MEDIA

The Daughters of St. Paul operate book and media centers at the following addresses. Visit, call, or write the one nearest you today, or find us at www.paulinestore.org.

CALIFORNIA

3908 Sepulveda Blvd, Culver City, CA 90230 — 310-397-8676
3250 Middlefield Road, Menlo Park, CA 94025 — 650-562-7060

FLORIDA

145 S.W. 107th Avenue, Miami, FL 33174 — 305-559-6715

HAWAII

1143 Bishop Street, Honolulu, HI 96813 — 808-521-2731

ILLINOIS

172 North Michigan Avenue, Chicago, IL 60601 — 312-346-4228

LOUISIANA

4403 Veterans Memorial Blvd, Metairie, LA 70006 — 504-887-7631

MASSACHUSETTS

885 Providence Hwy, Dedham, MA 02026 — 781-326-5385

MISSOURI

9804 Watson Road, St. Louis, MO 63126 — 314-965-3512

NEW YORK

64 W. 38th Street, New York, NY 10018 — 212-754-1110

SOUTH CAROLINA

243 King Street, Charleston, SC 29401 — 843-577-0175

TEXAS

Currently no book center; for parish exhibits or outreach evangelization, contact: 210-569-0500, or SanAntonio@paulinemedia.com, or P.O. Box 761416, San Antonio, TX 78245

VIRGINIA

1025 King Street, Alexandria, VA 22314 — 703-549-3806

CANADA

3022 Dufferin Street, Toronto, ON M6B 3T5 — 416-781-9131

¡También somos su fuente para libros,
videos y música en español!

Smile ☞ God Loves you